DEAD MAN'S EYES

Ex-train robber Jim Jackson is fresh out of the tough Texas Convict Leasing System, where brutal guards beat all the courage out of him. Now good for nothing except drinking, Jackson is known as 'Junk' by the townsfolk of Parker's Crossing. But Jackson has one thing going for him — he's the fastest gun the Texas Rangers have ever seen. When a series of violent murders terrify the people of Parker's Crossing, it is to Junk Jackson they turn. But can Jackson find the courage to take on the killers?

DEREK RUTHERFORD

---◆---

DEAD
MAN'S
EYES

Complete and Unabridged

LINFORD
Leicester

First published in Great Britain in 2016 by
Robert Hale
an imprint of The Crowood Press
Wiltshire

First Linford Edition
published 2019
by arrangement with
The Crowood Press
Wiltshire

A catalogue record for this book is available
from the British Library.

ISBN 978–1–4448–4177–0

Published by
F. A. Thorpe (Publishing)
Anstey, Leicestershire

Set by Words & Graphics Ltd.
Anstey, Leicestershire
Printed and bound in Great Britain by
T. J. International Ltd., Padstow, Cornwall

This book is printed on acid-free paper

1

Amos Dunkley, the man whose eyelids the Apache had sliced off, once said to Jim Jackson that, blind or not, he could see that Jim was a man of courage, that somewhere inside him courage still lived.

Jim Jackson had downed a glass of whiskey, his hands trembling, and said, 'They beat every ounce of courage out of me in Texas, Amos. But it's good of you to try and make me feel better.'

Now he realized that Amos mightn't have been wholly wrong. There wasn't much courage left. But there was enough. There *had* to be enough.

Someone — two people — were following him.

Jim had long known this day would come — had expected it sooner, to be honest — and had made plans accordingly. But planning was one thing, actually *doing* was another.

He could hear the snap of dry branches as they tracked him through the woods ten miles north of Parker's Crossing. He looked back over his shoulder repeatedly but could see nothing, just the trees and shafts of morning sunlight bursting through the canopy and illuminating the dusty air. But they were there. The cracking of those dry branches, and once or twice, the distant snort of a horse, giving them away. Earlier a whisper had carried forward to him on the down-slope winds. Maybe there were more than two. What then? How much courage did he have? Would his plans work out if there were four or five following him?

He worked his way down from the high ground, the woods thinning, and he emerged from the tree line, the New Mexico sun hot on his face. Ahead of him a wide valley, dry and brown, stretched towards more wooded slopes. Dotted across the valley were abandoned huts, here and there small groups of larger buildings, also abandoned, and on the far side, the mine buildings that had brought him here.

He eased his horse down the slope, leaving a trail of crushed grass. The grass had a blue sheen to it. He had never seen such grass anywhere else on his travels. The mine had a sign, no longer hanging but leaning against the old office building, that read *Santiago's Copper*. The folks back in the Crossing called this place Santiago when they called it anything, which was rare. But he had christened it Bluegrass in his own mind. It made it feel like a place that was private to him.

That was pretty much how it had been until this morning.

He resisted the urge to look over his shoulder as he worked his way into the deserted settlement. He wanted to reach back and pull his Remington shotgun from its scabbard and load a shell. But little good that would do against two of them. In fact, little good would it do against just one of them unless he were no more than twenty feet away.

He rode past the old saloon (*McCourey's* painted in sun-bleached orange above a door that squeaked in the breeze) and started working his way up the far slope to the cluster of mine buildings. There he swung off his horse and, still resisting the urge to look back, he looped the horse's reins over a wooden rail, stepped up onto the planking in front of the office building, pushed open the door and stepped inside.

From the dark safety within Jim Jackson turned and looked out of the dusty window. He could see the line of crushed grass he had left leading all the way back across the settlement, up the slope, and way over there, where he had emerged from the woods he saw two riders looking down upon him.

His heart quickened. He shuddered. It felt as if two huge cold fists had wrapped themselves around his spine and were squeezing his bones. He swallowed and found only trail dust in his mouth and yet the palms of his hands were greasy with sweat.

Two riders, no doubt violent men, or men prepared to do violence. They would have guns: revolvers. What good was his ancient Remington? And anyway he had left it out there on the back of his saddle.

He thought back to Amos telling him that there was still courage inside of him. Doubts crept in again, as they always did. Amos had been wrong. All that was inside of Jim Jackson was fear. That's why they called him Trembles or Shaky. That's why they called him Junk Jackson, because he was useless.

He gritted his teeth, felt the dust in his mouth.

No. He was better than that. He was more than the town drunk.

He forced himself to breathe deeply, to hold the breath, to try and calm his racing heart.

They were here after his money.

He let out his breath, slowly and deliberately, through pursed lips.

This Godforsaken land had stripped everything else from him — his woman, his pride, his courage, even his good years. The money was all he had left in this world.

And he was damned if they were going to take it.

* * *

'The guy is as much a fool as he is a waste of space,' Blue Garner said. 'How he's even still alive is a mystery.'

'You ain't wrong,' Henry Slade said. 'But we're fools too, yeah?'

'How do you figure?'

'We should have done this months ago. We could already be living the easy life like Junk does. Sleeping and drinking and maybe getting a poke once in a while.'

'I guess so.'

'Come on, let's see where he hides his money.'

The two men eased their horses out of the tree line and worked their way towards the abandoned settlement. Halfway down the slope Henry pressed

6

his spurs hard into his horse's side to encourage her to move faster. He didn't want to get down to the mine just as Junk was coming out with a handful of silver dollars. He wanted to be there in time to see where the fool hid his fortune. He didn't want to have to beat that knowledge out of the man. Far easier just to watch him.

'How much money you think he's got stashed away?' Blue said, as they skirted the old saloon.

'He never seems bothered about finding work,' Henry said. 'So I figure he's got enough to give us a good life for a long time.'

'First thing I'm going do is have me Li'l Lil for a whole night.'

Henry laughed and said, 'You'll be wasting about eight hours' worth of good money then.'

'What you saying?'

'I'm saying it's time to focus on the job in hand. Come on. Let's go and get rich, yeah?'

The two men dismounted outside the

mine building into which Junk Jackson had disappeared minutes earlier. They tied their horses alongside Junk's mare. Blue Garner pulled a Spencer repeating rifle from his saddle scabbard and Henry Slade drew his Colt revolver. Junk Jackson's horse whinnied as if she knew something was not right.

'Might be dark in there,' Blue said, looking at the grubby windows of the building. The office was built close to the side of the valley wall. Beyond the office other linked buildings spread out, some pressing right up against the rock. 'We should have brought candles.' There was a hint of nervousness in his voice.

'Junk's gotta see. He'll have some torches burning, I'd bet.'

'Yeah. Reckon so. Hope so.'

Henry held his gun out in front of him and stepped up to the door. The ancient planking beneath his feet creaked a little, but it felt solid.

'Junk's a fool.' Blue laughed. 'Look, he hasn't even taken that shotgun of his with him.'

Henry looked back at Junk's horse. Sure enough, there was his single shot Remington. 'I bet it would blow back anyway. You ever seen him use it?'

'Nope. Reckon it's just for show.'

'And he doesn't have a six-gun.'

'Nope.'

Henry said, 'He's a fool for sure. Let's go get him.'

He pushed open the door and stepped inside.

Jim Jackson heard his horse whinny. She always did a funny snorting thing half way through a whinny as if snatching an extra bit of air in order to keep the noise going. It meant he was able to recognize her by sound alone. Not that he'd ever needed to before. But now that noise sent his heart racing again.

They were coming for him.

A door at the back of the office led into a large storage area. The floor here was un-boarded, left exposed to the hard-packed ground. The area was big enough that there was an old flat wagon next to a set of double doors, doors that were locked on the inside by a huge beam of wood resting in iron brackets. Small windows above the doors let in thin streams of dusty light. Strewn around the room were picks and shovels, and sacks. On a table over by another set of wide doors were candles and a pair of kerosene lamps. Jim Jackson had been tempted to take the lamps back to Parker's Crossing and present them to Rose, his landlady. Rose would love them, but in doing so he'd have to explain where he got them. So he'd left them be, along with the chairs and hammers and bags of nails and even a good pair of working boots he'd found. Jim had always figured that had he needed work, he could have done worse than simply bring back to the Crossing all the abandoned items he'd found in Santiago and sell them on. A man could make a fortune if he cared to.

The second set of doors led into the valley wall itself. Beyond the doors was a short corridor, walled and roofed with wood, and then the darkness of a tunnel hewn into the rock. Jim had always suspected that this entrance was actually a natural cave, but the buildings prevented him from standing back and seeing the situation from a distance. There were no wooden struts, bracing, or supports until much further inside where the shafts got a little smaller. Smaller and narrower and a whole lot more labyrinthine.

Jim Jackson lit a kerosene lamp and placed it halfway along the cave section of the mine. The kerosene was old and impure and the lamp flickered and spluttered. But it illuminated the way to the back of the cave where the mine shafts were clearly hand-hewn. Crouching, he headed into the longest of these shafts. He lit torches about thirty feet apart along the shaft. On the ground, in one of the circles of shifting light from the burning torches, he carefully placed a silver dollar coin.

He crouched in that shaft now, and

he heard his horse whinny again, the sound distant and muffled, but unmistakable. He heard the squeak of door hinges and felt the whisper of a breeze on his face, and he felt those cold fists squeeze his spine once more. Here in the semi-darkness, deep underground, all the fear and terror and pain of what happened in Texas seemed to hover around him, almost touching him, like a ghost that could suddenly become real and carry him back to hell again.

He breathed deeply, the air cold and dry, and he held that breath.

He again felt the movement of air around his face.

He heard them whispering.

They were coming for him.

★   ★   ★

Blue Garner said, 'Heck, this is huge. I ain't never seen a mine this big.'

'Reckon this bit is a cave,' Henry Slade said.

They were standing just inside the

12

door to the mine. Jim Jackson's kerosene lamp illuminated the cavern and cast dark shadows around the walls that made the space look even greater.

Blue looked back over his shoulder. The entrance to the cave had been walled up with planking, save for the wide door through which they'd come.

'Figure old Santiago wanted to keep this place to himself,' Blue said. The sense of wonder was tinged with a little fear. There wasn't a whole lot of daylight in the mine.

'Yep,' Henry said, and for a second Blue thought he'd said something aloud about the darkness.

'I ain't sure I could have worked in a place like this,' Blue said. He could feel the weight of all that rock above him, and the cave itself felt a whole lot colder and darker than any regular night. There were ruts in front of him where hand carts or something similar had worn grooves into the hard ground.

'That's why it was run by a Mexican. They don't mind working. Anyway,'

Henry said, 'the fact is we're here for easy money. Come on.'

Blue let Henry go first. They walked deeper into the mine. It only took twenty paces and they were beyond the kerosene lamp and their bodies were now blocking the light, their shadows dancing on the walls. With each step Blue felt like his shoulders were supporting a little more of the weight of all that rock. He found himself breathing faster and louder. He looked over his shoulder repeatedly, checking that the light was still there.

'Shush,' Henry said, holding up a hand. 'Listen.'

Ahead of them there were three tunnel entrances hewn into the rock face. Two were pitch black, one was illuminated by a burning torch.

From within the lit-up tunnel they could hear the sound of a man gently humming to himself.

'Come on,' Henry said. 'And mind your head.'

'We have to go in there?' Blue said.

The tunnel looked too small for him to fit into. 'Those Mexicans weren't as big as us.'

'You want a whole night with Lil or not?'

Henry ducked into the shaft. A moment later Blue followed him, his spurs tinkling, his breathing audible, and his neck aching as he bent over. He could feel sweat rolling down his flanks even though it was pretty darn cold down there. Damn Junk for hiding his money in such a place.

A few moments later, just around a slight bend in the tunnel, Henry stopped and Blue bumped into him, his Spencer rifle digging into Henry's leg.

'Watch where you're going,' Henry hissed. 'And keep your finger off the damn trigger. A ricochet down here could kill us both.'

'What is it?' Blue said. He didn't want to stop. He wanted to get this done with. Get in there and grab Junk's stash and get the hell out. Luckily there was a torch burning in a metal cage in an alcove that someone had long ago chiselled out of the wall. The heat against his face was hot yet the rest of his body was shivering. At least it wasn't so dark right here. But then the light illuminated the old wooden struts that surely couldn't be strong enough to hold all this rock up.

Henry reached his hand backwards towards Blue. In his palm was a silver dollar.

For a moment the fear vanished. Blue looked at that coin and he imagined Li'l Lil and he could taste all the whiskey and the steaks over at the Pit and he knew that these few moments of discomfort would be worth it.

'Take it,' Henry said.

'You sure?'

'Going to be a whole lot more.'

They could still hear Junk Jackson humming a tune ahead of them.

'Come on, and watch out. It gets narrower and lower ahead. And for darn's sake mind that trigger.'

They inched forward. The silver coin

in his left hand gave Blue courage but he hit his head on a jagged rock and he cursed and felt blood. Then he scraped his shoulder on a sharp outcrop and felt his shirt tear. And as the shaft narrowed his shoulders hurt more and the straps of his leather chaps cut into his legs and it was getting darker because both their bodies cut out the light from the torch they had passed, and though there was a second torch ahead of them it flickered and Blue was sure it was on the point of dying.

'I ain't sure I can breathe too good,' Blue whispered.

'It's your imagination,' Henry said ahead of him. 'Besides, I can feel a breeze.' Then he added, 'Anyways, we're here.'

* * *

The ladder had been in the storage area the first time Jim Jackson had explored Santiago's mine. He'd found the settlement by pure chance back in the dark days when he'd been running from Texas. He spent a few weeks in the settlement, sleeping in the old saloon, eating wild onions, potatoes, and rabbit, and exploring. Once he'd found the main mine shaft and discovered that there was a natural air vent — big enough for a man to climb down — in the last chamber, the seeds of his plan had been set. Even if he hadn't known at the time that he'd need a plan.

That natural air vent would have been a godsend to Santiago once his shafts, following the copper seams, had connected to that natural large cavern deep inside the rock. Santiago's miners had worked that seam, expanding the cavern, and all the while nice fresh air was coming down from that hole in the cavern roof and blowing back towards the entrance. With the double doors wide open back there, it couldn't have been more perfect. All these years later, Jim Jackson could imagine Santiago smiling at his good fortune and thinking to himself, it's almost like it was meant to be.

Up on the rock face outside, no more than fifty yards from the entrance to the mine, the opening to that air hole was on a small ridge, where the valley walls were still rising. Thing was, if you hadn't known that air shaft existed you would have never looked for it, and certainly never found it.

Jim Jackson had discovered that he could drop that ladder down from the outside, even though he hadn't been able to drag it through the shaft itself on account of the twists and turns were too tight.

When he'd placed that ladder into the chamber the first time, he still hadn't really known what was on his mind. He'd known he was looking for a hiding place for the two large saddlebags of money he'd risked his life for. He'd known that if he was crawling about in an abandoned mine then having a way out other than the main entrance might be a wise thing. But he'd never really thought about using it as a trap.

Such thoughts arrived later when he came to understand that sooner or later someone would cotton on to the fact that he appeared to have an endless source of dollars and that someone might want to take those dollars from him.

He climbed up that ladder now, humming an old song to himself. It had been one of Jennifer Anne's favourites — 'Jeanie with the Light Brown Hair'. He'd never heard the song until he'd met Jennifer Anne, and the lyrics — which were always sad, even in those good days — made him terribly melancholy. The song was all about missing someone — Jeanie. It might as well have been called 'Jennifer With the Light Brown Hair'. Most of the time he tried not to think of Jennifer Anne. He had tried to train his mind not to go there. It wasn't easy. But he figured if a good horseman could train a wild stallion then he ought to be able to train his mind. Most of the time it worked. It was just in moments of stress that she came to mind. After all, everything that had followed was because of Jennifer Anne.

Now he squeezed himself up that air shaft and once at the top he pulled the ladder up, and then he slid a flat rock over the opening. From the inside now there'd be no light, no clue that the shaft even existed.

Then he ran along the small ridge, dropped down a number of natural rock steps, and scrabbled down the final few yards of the slope.

He ran back to Santiago's mine building, and re-entered, trying to slow and quieten his breathing. He was the one doing the following now, and didn't want to be heard.

★   ★   ★

Blue Garner wasn't exactly sure what happened. He emerged from that tiny shaft, still bent over, his shoulders, neck, and legs hurting and the darkness and all that rock feeling like it was closing in on him, making it hard to breathe, into a bigger chamber illuminated by just a single flickering torch on the wall. The cavern felt — because much of it was in darkness — as big as the eating room back at the Pit. The relief at being in a space so large was palpable. He stood up straight and felt something click in his right knee. He rolled his neck. He looked around and found himself taking a long deep breath. That tunnel had been tiny, he realized now. His head still hurt where he had caught it on the rock.

He knew he was going to have to go back out that way, too.

The fear started to edge back.

'He ain't here,' Henry Slade said.

'What?'

The torch flame was very low, as if it too was struggling to breathe. A little light came from the torch back in the tunnel. But in the tiny amount of light available they could see no-one else in the cavern.

'Come on out, Junk?' Henry said, his

Colt held out in front of him, his whole body turning as he worked his eyes around the room.

'He's hiding in the shadows,' Blue said. The chamber was large enough, high enough, and plenty dark enough that Shaky could still be in there. He *had* to be in there. Where else could he be?

'Shush,' Henry said.

Blue held his breath.

The silence was total. If Junk or Trembles or Shaky, call him what you will, was in that cave then he too was holding his breath.

They waited. They waited so long that Blue had to breathe again. He tried to do it as quietly as possible.

'He ain't here,' Henry said.

'He never passed us, that's for sure.'

'Then there must be another tunnel.'

'I ain't going down another tunnel.'

'You want this money or not?'

'I ain't sure I want it this bad.'

Henry slid his Colt back into his holster and walked over to the burning torch that had been forced into a crevice in the side of the cave. He pulled the torch free and holding it in front of him, he started to work his way around the chamber walls. There were a number of shafts that were clearly man-made but the first few only went into the rock face a matter of feet. There was one, just a deep black hole in the wall that looked like the sort of place where snakes or worse might live. It was deep enough that Blue couldn't see the end when Henry held the torch in front of it. But it was low to the ground, just about two feet high, and didn't look big enough for anyone to get in. Yet on the ground a yard into that shaft there was another dollar coin.

'I ain't going in there,' Blue said. 'No darn way.'

'Your big head wouldn't fit in there,' Henry said.

'You think that's it? That's where he went?'

'He ain't here, is he?'

They quartered the rest of the

chamber, but the story was the same. Lots of workings but none leading to any other chamber.

'I don't hear him singing no more,' Blue said.

'No.'

'He can't have just disappeared.'

'Which leaves just one option.'

'No way,' Blue said.

Henry went back across the chamber to that tiny low shaft.

'Here, hold the torch.' Blue was still clutching that silver dollar in one hand and holding his Spencer in the other. He stuffed the coin in a pocket and took the torch from his partner.

Henry then got down on his back and started to wriggle into the cave and Blue felt his own belly start to tighten and churn; he felt his skin crawling with fear, and when he tried to swallow he found that he had no spit.

'Them Mexicans are a lot smaller than us,' Blue said.

When all that remained sticking out of the tiny hole was Henry Slade's feet, the torch back in the shaft they had come down flickered and died.

'No,' Blue said. 'Mother Mary, no.' The only light was the torch he now held. That torch felt very small and insignificant and his hand was all of a sudden slippery with moisture and what if he dropped it?

'Henry,' he said. 'You see anything? Henry?'

'Pull me out,' Henry said.

'Hold on.'

Blue found a crevice in the wall and worked the torch into it.

'Come on,' Henry said. 'Hurry up.'

Blue grabbed Henry's ankles and pulled him out of that tiny tunnel.

'We don't need to go through there, do we?' Blue said. The torch sent flickering shapes across Henry's dirty face. All around them was darkness. Blue was starting to figure that Shaky deserved that money if every time he needed some he had to go through all of this.

'It leads nowhere,' Henry said. 'He

ain't here. The money ain't here.'

'He must have gone somewhere. He ain't a ghost.'

Henry said nothing, he was looking around the cavern.

'He ain't a ghost, is he, Henry?' Blue asked.

Before Henry Slade could answer there came a deep rumbling sound, a sound that grew louder and louder, and Blue felt the pressure of air on his face and the sound grew stronger still and now he could taste dust in that air, feel the dust landing on his skin.

Then the sound was gone. All sound was gone.

'What was that?' Blue said.

'I'm no miner,' Henry said. 'But that sounded like a rock fall to me.'

2

Life would have been, Jim Jackson figured, a whole lot easier if he was a killer. Not being a killer had got him into a whole lot more trouble than being a killer ever would have. Take those two back there — he wasn't sure who they were, didn't recognize their horses — but if he'd have killed them, if he'd had set things up differently, which he could have done very easily, things would have been a whole lot easier.

He was going to have to leave town now. Leave Parker's Crossing and leave Amos and Li'l Lil and Rose. And where would he go? He couldn't go back to Texas — not in a million years would he go back to Texas. He didn't really want to head west through the mountains. Geronimo may well have finally surrendered, but that didn't mean there weren't still a few Apache out there

— and look at what they did to Amos.

He didn't want to go back East. Back East was where Jennifer Anne was, and though he wanted to see Jennifer Anne more than he wanted anything else in the world, that life had been a dozen years ago. Jennifer Anne would no doubt be married to a rich and well-heeled young man now, a handsome fellow with good connections and manners, and they'd probably have children and a big house and her husband would be on the board of one of her daddy's companies and seeing all of that would hurt more than anything they ever did to him in Texas. That just left the north. So the north it would be. But what was up north but rain and cold? No, it would have been a whole lot easier if he'd have killed them two back there.

After he'd crept back into the cave he had pulled down the wooden support that he'd laboriously set up across the entrance to that one shaft. The support had held up what felt like a ton of rocks and stone and grit, all of which had sealed up that tunnel entrance completely. They would, of course, be able to work their way out. But there wasn't much room in that shaft to shift those rocks out of the way. It might take all day. Maybe all day and all night. But they'd do it and then, of course, they'd come looking for him.

He'd untied their horses, but both horses had just stood there. Fine. If they cared to they could wait.

Then, still in Santiago, Jim Jackson had crossed to McCourey's old saloon and to the outhouse which was the perfect place to hide his money.

He had also hidden some money *within* the old saloon. He'd put enough money in a large glass jar that he'd hidden beneath floorboards in one of the downstairs rooms that if anyone found it, they would figure they'd discovered Jim's fortune and, hopefully, stopped looking, and thus never find his main stash.

Now he gathered all the money from

both hiding places and put it back in his saddlebags, just like when he'd left Texas. He was feeling nervous again. He'd have to move on and he'd have to find a new home and new hiding places and it would have been a whole lot easier if he'd have been a killer.

Especially considering he'd already done ten years of very hard time for being one.

★ ★ ★

That afternoon, in Parker's Crossing, someone found a body.

Riding back into town from the north, Jim Jackson came across a commotion in the area behind the Domino Saloon. There was a crowd gathered and Jim could pick out Sheriff Wagner calling for calm. Julio Ramez, the sheriff's deputy, was trying to hold folks back from a flat-bed wagon.

'Where you been, Shaky?' Little Joe Grubber asked, trotting alongside Jim's horse.

31

Joe was no more than eight or nine years old. He had no knowledge of why they called Jim Shaky. Or Trembles. Or Junk. Though one time Little Joe did ask Jim why he trembled so much. 'I feel the cold,' Jim had told him.

'Been riding round,' Jim said, looking down at Little Joe. Joe was wearing a yellow felt hat. It was his pride and joy, despite being too big for him and needing to be filled out with screwed up paper to sit on top of his head and prevent it sliding down over his eyes. Little Joe often told how the hat had once belonged to an outlaw called Dark Johnson who had been hanged for rustling sheep. Jim asked him, 'What's happening up ahead?'

'They found a dead man.'

'Who?' Jim had seen plenty of dead men in his time, had dug many a grave, and once or twice had even been the one who had first come across the bodies. That was Texas for you.

'Who found him? I don't know.'

'No, who is it?'

'Don't know that, either. I heard Missy Mulligan saying there was too much blood to tell. I'll find out soon.'

'I know you will. You find out everything. But don't go trying to get a look,' Jim said. 'You're liable to get nightmares.'

'I'm not scared of no dead man.'

Jim smiled. Amos and Lil and Rose aside, Little Joe Grubber was probably the only other person for whom he held any affection in the Crossing.

'You hot?' Little Joe asked him.

'Hot?' It was always hot in New Mexico. Especially by the late afternoon.

'Yeah, hot.'

'No more than usual.'

'You're not shaking,' Little Joe said, and ran off towards the flatbed.

Jim walked his horse slowly around the crowd. Someone was crying and somebody else was laughing. Mostly folks were just talking. A few people looked in his direction but as always their glances tended to sweep over him as if he wasn't there or wasn't worth bothering with. From his position on his horse he was able to see the body laid out on the back of the wagon and the doc there alongside Wagner. The doc was wiping blood off the dead man's face with a cloth that he dipped into a pail of water.

'It's Southee Bell,' someone said, as the blood mask was removed. The words rippled back across the crowd like wind blowing through prairie grass. Southee Bell ran the hardware store over behind the Pit. It would have been to Southee that Jim Jackson would have taken all those abandoned items back in Santiago.

'Who'd want to kill Southee?'

'He was a good man. Didn't deserve this.'

'Why in hell's name would someone kill Southee?'

As he rode past the crowd Jim heard someone say, 'I told you this would happen. I told you there was trouble in town.'

He looked around but he couldn't see who had spoken. Then he was riding away from the crowd and the dead man and he turned into Main Street and it was quiet, almost deserted, on account of everyone was back there behind the Domino. A dog scratched its ear over in the shade by the sheriff's office and a couple of ladies, not ladies from the Domino but respectable ladies, stood further along the plank walk.

Jim Jackson rode down to the livery where he left his horse with Mannie and then, as nonchalantly as he could, he heaved his heavy saddlebags over his shoulder, grabbed his Remington and headed back to Rose's.

He needed to pack his few belongings, pay his bills, and say his goodbyes.

★   ★   ★

Amos said, 'What's happening out there, Jim?'

'How did you know it was me?' Jim

35

said. He was still ten yards from Amos, who was outside Rose's boarding house leaning on the railing and looking sightlessly down Main Street. Amos had, as usual, a damp and slightly dirty bandage wrapped around his head and over his eyes. He had a couple of those bandages and did his best to keep them clean but the dampness attracted dust like a dog attracts fleas. Amos tried to keep that bandage damp all day long. He reckoned as long as it was damp his eyes didn't hurt so much, and who knew, maybe one day he'd see again.

'You favour one of your legs,' Amos said. 'I don't know which one. But one spur clinks a little louder than the other.'

'No-one else in town with the same affliction?'

'None that boards with Rose.'

Jim came and stood alongside Amos and stared down Main Street, too. He had become Amos's eyes. The old frontier man, with his white hair and sharp mind, had come to rely on Jim.

And although Amos had got by just fine before Jim had arrived in town, and would no doubt get by after he had left, it still raised a feeling of guilt within. Hell, he was only halfway through *Moll Flanders*, some of which he read to Amos most nights before he went out drinking. Or rather, if he was honest, *between* bouts of drinking.

'Seems like someone killed Southee Bell,' Jim said. 'They found his body back of the Domino. Someone cut him up good.'

'Southee Bell,' Amos said.

'The hardware man.'

'I know who he is. Damn fool never paid 'em, did he?'

'Never paid who?'

Amos turned and looked at Jim Jackson. Jim had long got used to the blind man with the bandage over his eyes looking right at him as if he could still see.

'If I knew that, I'd go and tell Sheriff Wagner and he could arrest them and everyone would be happy again.'

'I have no idea what you're talking about.'

'No. I guess you don't.'

'What's that meant to mean, Amos?'

'You know they're coming after Rose, too?'

'Who?'

'Like I said, if I knew that, I'd go and tell Sheriff Wagner. He could arrest them and we'd all be happy again.'

'Someone's threatening Rose?'

'Uh-huh.'

'And you never told me?'

The bandaged eyes turned away from Jim and stared back towards where the sound of the crowd, out of sight but still noisy, floated towards them on the hot breeze.

'What would you do, Jim? What would you have done?'

Amos's tone wasn't designed to hurt, but did so anyway.

Jim Jackson felt a dampness in his own eyes. He was glad, just for a moment, that Amos was unable to see him. How had it come to this? How could a life once so full of dreams and hope end up like this? Was he nothing but a drunken coward looked down upon even by his only friend?

Jim Jackson stood with his shotgun in one hand and the heavy saddlebags digging painfully into his shoulder supported by the other hand. He took that hand away from the saddlebags now and held it out in front of him.

He was trembling again.

Little Joe Grubber had told him he wasn't shaking — and for a short moment in time that had been true. What he had done back there in Santiago had invigorated him, had made him feel . . . if not good, then at least capable.

But it had only been for a short moment of time.

Back here, alongside Amos, with the truth settling back upon him, the trembles — the fear — were back.

It wasn't his fault. He understood that. What they'd done to him . . . it would break any man. But the way he reacted to it, the way he hid from it, *that* was down to him. And in Amos's voice he heard condescension and pity and shame.

'I didn't know,' he said when he was able to speak. 'About Rose, I mean.'

The bandaged eyes turned towards him.

'I'm sorry, Jim. We've all got demons to deal with, don't we? It's just . . . '

'Just what?'

'If I could still see, I'd like to think I might try and help Rose. That's all.'

Jim looked out along Main Street. A few people were drifting back into sight now as the initial excitement and activity over the discovery of Southee's body waned. Or, looking at them, maybe the excitement hadn't waned, maybe those folks simply needed a drink. Most of them were headed straight for the Domino. Jim could feel his body, his belly, his arms, his neck, his shoulders, all calling out for him to join them. He needed a drink, too. He needed a drink more than any of them.

'I never told you much about Texas, did I?' he said to Amos.

'Nope. Aside from the fact they beat whatever courage you once had out of you. You told me that much every time you were drunk and maudlin. Which was . . . ' Amos let the words hang.

'Which was what, Amos?'

'Nothing.'

'No, go on.'

'It don't matter.'

'Yes it does.'

'No, it — '

'You were going to say *every day*, weren't you? Every time I'm drunk, which is every day.'

'It's the truth.'

'I know, I wish . . . '

'It is what it is,' Amos said. 'As I said, we've all got our demons.'

Jim paused, thinking about how he'd ended up in such a place. He said, 'They beat me it seemed like every day. With the bat.'

'The bat?'

'It's a leather strap attached to a long

41

wooden handle.'

'Uh-huh.'

'Maybe it doesn't sound much. You know what it can do to a man? You scream. You can't help but scream. They strip you and they hold you down — well, they get your fellow convicts to keep you down — and every blow feels like they're stripping skin off you.' Jim paused. His hands were shaking even more. Saying this stuff out loud was bringing it back more clearly than when he kept it in. That said, it did feel good to share it just a little. He'd never really told Amos — or anyone — much about his past. He saw more people heading into the saloon. More than anything he wanted a drink. 'Most times they did actually strip skin from you. They had it down to a fine art.'

Amos said nothing.

'You could hear the screams from a hundred, two hundred, yards away. See, most of the time the threat of the bat was enough. You only had to have it once or twice and they'd got you where they wanted you. You did what you were told. But for some reason they beat me whenever and *why*ever. It got so bad I wanted to die. I was scared to put one foot in front of the other in case I was placing it wrong.'

Amos nodded. 'They broke you.'

'It was agony. But it was humiliating, too. You can't control yourself. Not in that much pain. It changes you. I wasn't always . . . Junk.'

'Why were you in prison in the first place?'

'They say I killed a man.'

'Say?'

'I didn't do it. I'm not a killer.' Saying those words reminded Jim of his feelings earlier and how, had he been a killer, he could have avoided having to leave town. But then how could he leave now anyway? With Rose in trouble and Amos practically ordering him to get his act together and to help on account of at least he could see. But what would happen when those two finally dug themselves out of the mine and came back to Parker's Crossing?

'Why did they single you out the way they did?'

'I guess I don't know. I did hear the fellow they said I killed was a Texas Ranger. It wasn't good — the killing, I mean. There was no need. But it wasn't me that did it. Or maybe because I was a well-spoken Eastern fellow. They used to call me Gentleman Jim. I stood up for my rights — before I realized I didn't have any. I spoke up for other convicts. One of them reckoned they were trying to push me so hard I'd make a run for it and then they could shoot me. Said they wanted me dead.'

'So they made every day hell and you're still suffering?'

'That's about the size of it, Amos. I'm sorry.'

The two men were silent for a while, then Amos said, 'You know what happened to me?'

'It was the Apache, wasn't it?'

'Chiricahua. They attacked my farm. They killed my wife and children and they staked me down in the sun and they cut my eyelids off.'

'Amos — '

Amos shook his head, 'It was a long time ago. But you know, Rose, she won't take a nickel off me, and she feeds me and she gives me a place to stay. You read to me, Jim. Folks talk to me. They ain't all bad and you can't live in the past even though every day the past is going to try and grab you. It'll eat you up from the inside out. You think every morning when I wake up I don't remember exactly what happened? But I fight it, Jim. And if I had eyes I'd fight for Rose, too.' Amos paused, then added, 'Think about it, Jim. Think about who you are, who you were, and who you want to be.'

★   ★   ★

Connery said, 'You're drinking slow tonight, Junk.'

'I've a lot on my mind.'

'What's new? Figured that's why you

always drank fast rather than slow.'

'Maybe things have changed.'

Connery was serving behind the bar at the Domino. The saloon was owned by three fellows from Kansas. Once in a while they even made the journey West, usually on the look out for new investments and — so Connery said — for a few weeks away from their wives.

'Things have changed, huh?' Connery looked at him, tilting his head and raising his eyebrows as if to suggest disbelief.

Jim Jackson lifted his whiskey glass and took just a sip. It was hardly enough to do more than set his lips tingling. His hand was shaking as he put the glass down and it felt like every nerve ending in his body was crying out for that alcohol. But Amos's words had cut deep. If Amos could live with the past then maybe so could he.

'Talking of change, there's a fellow over by the door staring at you,' Connery said. 'New in town. Don't recognize him.'

The mirror behind Connery's bar

was dirty and the silver had come off in places but Jim could make out the man that Connery was referring to. A big fellow, bearded, sitting at the table by the door where the last of the evening sunlight painted him orange. He had a glass of whiskey on the table, the bottle too, and he was just sitting there quietly watching the rest of the folks in the saloon. There was the usual crowd in, although the piano that those Kansas fellows had brought with them last time they visited was sitting closed and quiet in the corner. Maybe later, Amy, one of the Domino girls who had a way with music as well as men, might sit down and play.

Meanwhile, all of the talk was about Southee Bell. Simply standing at the bar, listening, it was possible to build several theories about what had happened. On balance it turned out that what Amos had said was the most likely truth. Someone had demanded money of Southee, he hadn't paid, and now he was dead. There was a body of opinion that the guys behind it had set up in the Bridge Hotel at the far end of town. Supposedly the gang sat in the lounge and had guards on the doors so that no-one could get close. One fellow said he'd just come from the Bridge and there was nothing like that going on.

Another said, 'You won't see it. They don't look like guards, but they're there.'

Someone else said that Southee had been unlucky. 'He was the message,' this fellow said, 'that those guys wanted to send out.'

Another cowboy asked Connery if he'd been approached. 'I'm always being approached by folks wanting what I got for nothing.' He reached down behind the bar and came up with a pick-handle. 'My message is always the same. You have to pay or leave.' He smiled and the men had laughed, and in the mirror, Jim Jackson saw the bearded fellow stand up and start walking towards him.

'I need to leave,' Jim said to Connery.

He lifted his whiskey glass and downed the contents in one. That was better. *That* was how a drink was meant to be taken. Why was he pretending to think otherwise? Without turning or waiting for a reply from Connery, he pushed his way along the bar, through the crowd, ignoring a jibe that Junk was headed to the outhouse which was about where he belonged. He had no idea who the bearded man was, didn't recognize him, but that meant nothing and it didn't matter. Jim Jackson had no desire to meet anyone who wanted to meet him. The only way he could deal with the past was to avoid it totally. Whether or not this fellow was anything to do with that past it wasn't worth the risk.

He saw Li'l Lil at the top of the stairs as he pushed through to the back corridor that led outside. She smiled at him, her face lighting up and the skin around her green eyes crinkling. She really was the prettiest girl in the whole of Parker's Crossing. She waved, too, and he managed a quick smile back.

This was what he didn't want to lose — Lil and Amos, Rose, and Little Joe Grubber. It wasn't quite what you'd call a family, but it was better than anything he could have imagined during the last ten years.

He stepped outside, the air suddenly fresh and clean and reminding him how dense it was inside the Domino, the sweat and the whiskey and burning candles and oil lamps and the clothes that were never washed and all of it mingling into something you didn't notice until you went outside where the stars were visible in the darkening sky and the air was clean, even though the outhouse was just a few steps away.

He took a deep breath. His heart racing like it had done back in Santiago that morning.

His hands were trembling.

He'd been a fool. Amos had been right, he did need to think about who he was. And now he knew. He was Junk Jackson. He was Trembles. He was Shaky.

That was just the way it was.

Instead of walking along Main Street, he ducked down the alley behind the Domino — the alley where they'd found Southee Bell's body earlier — and he worked his way quickly back across town in the darkness and shadows behind Main Street's buildings.

He came out into the town square, where there were water troughs and a well, although the river ran close by and a lot of folks got their water there. They'd walk down to the gravel bar below the wooden bridge at the west end of town and fill up their buckets and jugs and skins. Little Joe Grubber even made his living that way. Running round all day long filling up water buckets for a nickel a time. Folks called him the 'water boy' and Little Joe even had several other boys working for him now, one of them a half-breed orphan that the 10th Cavalry had dumped on Father Thornley when they found the kid sitting by the bodies of his kin after a battle not far from Alma, or so Amos said. Supposedly, the kid's father had been Chiricahua and his mother had been a pretty white woman. When Father Thornley arrived in the Crossing he already had the kid in tow. All Little Joe Grubber said about the kid was that he had no name so Joe had christened him Ghost, and that even though he wasn't grown up he could track like a sniffer dog.

Amos said Ghost was a good name for the kid. 'You don't hear him coming,' he said once. 'Although he does smell Indian.' Amos also said that some folks weren't keen on an Apache bringing them water, even if the kid was half white. 'How about you?' Jim had asked. Amos had said, 'Little Joe himself brings Rose her water. And if he doesn't she gets it from the well.' And the tone in his voice had brought that particular conversation to a close.

Now Jim crossed the square, casting a quick glance back towards the lights of the distant Domino. There was no sign of the bearded man whom he had believed had been coming towards him. That was the thing, he thought, as he wandered over the hard rutted ground towards the Bridge Hotel and another drink, it was just a belief, just conjecture. The fellow may have simply been headed to the bar. But no, he'd had a bottle on the table and Connery had said the fellow had been staring at him. The fellow *had* been coming for him. There was no doubt about it. And whatever he wanted it wasn't anything that Jim wanted.

The Bridge Hotel was a step up in class from the Domino. Which was why Jim preferred the Domino. He could drink in the Domino until he couldn't drink any more. No matter what they thought of him there was usually someone there to help him home. Rose's boarding house was close, and Li'l Lil worked the Domino, too. All these things were in the Domino's favour.

The Bridge Hotel, with plush maroon

leather seats in the lounge and clean windows and folks all dressed well, it wasn't the same. It wasn't a place where a man could relax into a bottle of whiskey. Oh, they had a saloon bar there. It wasn't all leather seats and expensive women. There were fights in the bar the same as the Domino, but it was always a better class of fight. What was it that he'd read back when he was still yet to tread west of the Mississippi? The Marquess of Queensberry, over in London, had come up with a set of rules for fighting. Gentlemanly rules. Tim figured that, aside from him, there was probably no-one currently west of the Mississippi, let alone in Parker's Crossing, who had heard of these rules, but he figured they'd go down a lot better in the Bridge Hotel than they would in the Domino.

The other thing, of course, was they didn't like him in the Bridge Hotel. They tolerated him on a quiet night and they were happy to take his money. But they always made it clear that they thought he was a drunk, a waste of space, and a coward, too. It was they who coined the nickname Trembles for him, when to everyone else he'd been Junk.

'They' were Thomas Sanderson and his wife Ellie, who ran the place. Jim didn't know if they owned it or not, but they certainly dressed and acted like they did. Then there was Wolfgang — Jim didn't know his surname — who tended the bar, and there was a short guy, couldn't have been more than four feet tall, who Jim only knew as Big Mingus, who mopped and brushed and cooked and wore a Colt .45 with an ivory handle. Big Mingus was supposedly quick with that gun, although Jim had never seen him in action. They had girls, too. Pretty girls. Not that the girls over at the Domino weren't pretty. As far as Jim was concerned Li'l Lil was worth all of the Bridge girls put together, and then some. But there was no denying the girls at the Bridge dressed nice and smelled nice.

Thomas Sanderson often had other guys around the hotel, too. There was usually someone leaning on the bar watching out for trouble. Tonight there was also a fellow leaning on the wall by the door, a tall lean guy, slim hipped. It wasn't anyone Jim recognized. Jim Jackson thought back to the conversation he had overheard at the Domino just a few minutes earlier. Maybe there was some truth in the gossip.

The guy watched him as he pushed through the door and into the saloon.

Big Mingus was sitting on a tall wooden stool at the bar. He was drinking whiskey from a glass that sparkled in the golden light from a polished brass oil lamp hanging from the ceiling.

'Trembles,' he said, looking round. 'How brave of you to venture down town at night.'

'I just want a drink.'

'As always.'

Jim walked up to the bar. He was head, shoulders, and chest taller than

Big Mingus but somehow the little man made him feel small, insignificant, and not a little nervous.

'Whiskey,' he said to Wolfgang.

'Whiskey,' the barman said. He pronounced it *viskey*. '*Vhat* else is there for Trembles?'

'Kicked you out of the Domino, did they?' Mingus asked, looking up at him.

'I fancied a change of scenery.'

'They kicked you out.'

Wolfgang put a glass of whiskey on the polished bar in front of Jim. 'I pour you a large one. I know you like.'

Jim dug a dollar coin from his pocket and placed it on the bar. Wolfgang let it sit there. The Bridge Hotel was that kind of place. When Jim picked up the drink his hand was shaking.

'Trembles,' Mingus said, and it felt like the whole of Jim Jackson's world was summed up in that one word.

Jim downed half the drink in a single swallow. It burned his throat. When he put the glass back down his hand was steadier. At least he thought it was, *hoped* it was. He picked the glass back up and finished the drink. Then he nodded at Wolfgang for a refill.

'Trembles,' Mingus said. 'You drink like no-one else in this town. Where you get your money, Trembles? You don't do no work.'

There it was again. A subtle pressure that he could feel in the back of his neck. Someone else alluding to his money — although those two this morning hadn't been merely alluding to it, they'd been actively looking to take it off him. It really was time to skip town. Next time he'd have to think about how to avoid the suspicion of riches. Here in Parker's Crossing all he'd thought about was drinking enough to keep his memories at bay. Anything else had been something for another day.

He ignored Big Mingus's question and he turned and cast an eye around the room.

The saloon was busy. A group of well-dressed fellows played cards at one table, the doc was sat talking earnestly with one of the Bridge girls at another. A line of men, some talking, some just drinking, stood at the bar itself. Meredith, who ran the newspaper and the parcel office, was chatting to a silver headed man in a suit complete with vest and gold watch chain, and over in the far corner, just like those rumours from the Domino had referred to, was a small group of men around a table.

It seemed to Jim that there was a fellow at the centre of the group, a smart fellow, maybe a businessman, but there was something about his face — a hardness that spoke of something else. He had a knife scar running from his cheek back up behind his eye and into the shadow of his smart black hat. The way he sat, just the shape of his body in the chair reminded Jim of some of the guards back in Texas. Guys that would sit there holding forth, laughing, seemingly having a good time one minute, and the every next minute they'd hit you behind the ear with an iron bar and drag you outside for a beating. Usually for no reason. It was folks like that you didn't want to lock eyes with. Around this fellow, three other guys who somehow appeared soft and deferential, maybe even a little sycophantic. One of the three was standing and he looked younger and looked more like a cowboy or, God forbid, a gunslinger. He reminded Jim of the fellow outside leaning nonchalantly against the door frame.

'You have a rich mother?' Mingus said. 'She send you money?'

He looked back at the little man.

'Yes. That's exactly right.'

Mingus looked up at him. 'Are you serious?'

'Uh-huh.'

'Your mother want to buy me a drink? Maybe she like a poke later?' The little man started to laugh. Spittle flew from his mouth. 'You punch me if you want,' he said after his laughter had subsided. 'We can fight if you like?' he added, and started laughing again.

Jim Jackson was on his fourth large whiskey when someone put their hand on his shoulder. He turned and it was the bearded man from the Domino.

Fear flared within Jim. He recalled, not so many years ago, standing in line with his wooden bowl awaiting the evening's portion of beans, stale bread, and — if they were lucky — bacon fat when a guard had put his hand on Jim's shoulder and had said, 'Come with me, Jackson.'

'What have I done?' he'd asked. By then fear had already been coursing through his body. His hands had already started trembling, and he was having to squeeze his belly to keep his bodily functions under control. He knew what was coming.

'Boss said you took it easy today.'

'I worked harder than anyone.'

'Are you arguing?'

Jim knew that any excuse would serve to prolong, maybe double, the agony.

'No, sir.'

'Then come with me.'

The memory came flooding back with the touch of hand on shoulder and even before he'd focussed on the bearded man, Jim was twisting from his stool at the bar, standing, turning to run, but it felt like all that whiskey he'd drunk had gone to his feet and one of his boots got tangled in the legs of the barstool and then he was crashing to the ground, pulling over the stool and everybody was laughing and he heard someone saying, 'Trembles is drunk again,' and someone else said, 'What a waste of skin that man is,' and where his lip had hit the floor he could taste blood and on his buttocks could feel the slicing agony of those leather straps as they beat him again and again, and then the fellow with the beard was leaning down, helping him up, and saying, 'Jim Jackson, I believe?'

3

'I didn't recognize you,' Jim said. 'The beard.'

Had he recognized the man, whose name was Sam McRae, Jim feared he might not just have lain there tangled in the legs of the bar stool but also have scrabbled across the floor in terror. As it was the laughter and ridicule had only lasted a minute. God knew how long it would have gone on for had he tried to escape the man on his hands and knees.

The recognition came a few moments later when McRae was helping Jim to his feet. When Jim stiffened in fear McRae had been quick to say, 'It's OK, Jim. This time it's OK. I promise.'

They took a table across by the far wall, just beyond the card players. McRae bought a bottle of whiskey and two glasses and Jim felt a small amount of pleasure at the way Big Mingus was twisting in his chair, trying to figure out who this new guy was and what business he had with Trembles.

McRae was a large man, not fat, but with a breadth to his shoulders that suggested strength. He was tall and he sat with a stillness that spoke of a confidence that Jim Jackson could only dream of. McRae spoke quietly, his voice so low that Jim struggled to hear.

'You probably want to kill me,' he said.

'No. I mean, I don't know. I don't want to kill anyone. But . . . ' Maybe I do want to kill him, Jim thought. What this man had put him through. There was an anger — a fury, even — bubbling somewhere inside him. But it was held in check by confusion about what Sam was doing in Parker's Crossing, and by the way that Sam was treating him, talking to him. 'You know what they did to me?'

'Yes,' Sam McRae said.

'You do?'

'I heard. I need to apologize.'

The whiskey coursing through Jim's veins felt warm. The warmth served to enhance his confusion. It made him weary, too. It was hard to reconcile the friendliness of the fellow sitting with him, buying him drink, offering an apology, with the man who over ten years ago had brought him to justice.

'What you went through. No man should have to do that. I'm sorry.'

Jim lifted his whiskey and drank some more. McRae refilled both their glasses. Across the room Jim noticed that Sheriff Wagner was standing in front of — and pointing at — the scarred man. If Jim wasn't mistaken the sheriff was shaking a little, maybe with anger rather than fear. The scarred man seemed nonplussed. In fact he was smiling. The young gunman — as Jim had labelled him — even put an arm around the sheriff's shoulder. The sheriff shrugged him off.

He turned back to McRae. Seeing the sheriff's anger brought some of his own to the surface. 'Why apologize?

Was it all your fault?'

'No. I'm not apologizing because it was my fault. I'm apologizing on behalf of my state.'

'Texas.'

'No-one's asked me to. I just . . . Look, I never came searching for you. I saw you at the bar across town. You saw me and you ran. I knew then it was you and here I am. And I'm sorry.'

'No. No, it's not enough. It's not right. It's . . . I don't know.' It was beginning to get a little difficult for Jim to consistently formulate sentences. Whiskey, bad memories, and shock fogged his brain. 'An apology is easy. Too easy.'

McRae leant back in his chair. 'I just want you to know I'm sorry. It shouldn't have happened.'

'It changed . . . ruined . . . my life.'

'It's not over.'

A moment of fear again. 'What's not over?'

'Your life. I mean, it's not too late, is it?'

'For what?'

66

'To make your life what you want it to be.'

Jim drank some whiskey. He took a deep breath, tried to keep a lid on the rising anger, and said, 'You sound like Amos.'

'Amos?'

'A fellow I know.'

'Well, maybe Amos is right.'

'You still a Ranger?'

'Nope. Bounty hunter now.'

'Bounty hunter?'

'Yep.'

'I bet you're good. Sending many a feller to hell.'

Jim shook his head as if to pass judgement on McRae's profession. He picked up the fact that the sheriff had left the room and now several of the other folks in the group he'd been talking to — including the man at the centre of that particular gang — were looking over at him and McRae. He avoided eye contact with them.

'There's something else, too,' McRae said.

Jim still couldn't figure out his own feelings towards McRae. The man was different, genuinely friendly, and clearly seeking some kind of forgiveness. But how could you forgive a man for *that*?

'I know you never killed that fellow that they said you killed,' McRae said.

'He was a Ranger, too.'

'Yep.'

'Was that why Texas treated me the way it did?'

'Maybe. They don't like one of their own being . . . executed like that.'

'But it wasn't me.'

'That's what I said. I know.'

'I told you that back then. You never believed me. No-one believed me. That girl . . .'

Now Jim realized that the guys across the room weren't looking at him but were looking at McRae. He couldn't figure out why. How would they know McRae? Or was it simply because McRae was talking to him, Trembles Jackson? That was surely what was intriguing Big Mingus so much. Maybe it was the same with those others. Or perhaps they'd overheard McRae saying he was a bounty hunter. But no, he was still speaking in such a low voice they couldn't have done. Nevertheless they were unnerving him and Jim was beginning to wish he'd stayed in the Domino.

'What girl?' McRae said.

'The one from the train. At the trial.'

'She said you had a bandana covering your face.'

'She said it wasn't the gentleman who shot the Ranger. And you all knew I was the gentleman she was referring to. Gentleman Jim, they called me.'

'I know.'

'You know?'

'I know they called you Gentleman Jim.'

'You know I never killed anyone.'

'I know now.'

'You didn't know then?'

'It wasn't my job. The jury found you guilty. They believed.'

'You could have said something.'

'My job was to bring you in.'

The whiskey had gone from warming him to hurting him and the pain made him angry again. He tried to figure just what McRae was after and the only thing he could think of was to make himself — McRae — feel a little better about what he'd done all those years ago.

'Well, you bought me in and they sent me to hell. So I guess it was job done. Excuse me if I don't accept your apology.'

Jim stood up. His legs were unsteady but at least he didn't fall over this time.

'There's more,' McRae said.

'I've heard enough. You apologized. I listened. Now I'm going back to the Domino to be amongst friends.'

'Please sit down.'

'Thanks for the whiskey.'

Jim headed for the door. The floorboards felt a little unsteady beneath his feet and he had to hold his arms out for balance, but he was darned if he was going to fall over and give them all another laugh.

'Leaving us already,' Big Mingus said from his stool at the end of the bar. 'You come back soon. Tell us who that fellow is.'

Outside the cool clean air went straight to Jim's head and he found himself dizzy enough that he had to hold onto a post. There were two, no, three, moons in the sky and Main Street was at a very odd angle. He held onto that post for a while until he suspected his balance was as good as it was going to get, then he pushed himself off and aimed himself back towards the Domino. Almost immediately his foot caught one of the wheel ruts that had been baked into the hard ground and a moment later he hit the dirt, smashing his lip for the second time that evening. But this time there was no laughter, no insults, just a strong helping hand pulling him back up.

'I was only doing my job,' McRae said.

'Leave me alone.'

71

'I've something else to tell you, then I will go. I hope you remember it in the morning. I think it's important.'

'It's important that you leave me alone.'

Together they started weaving their way up Main Street, McRae holding Jim Jackson upright, guiding him towards the Domino.

'It's important that you know — '

'What?'

'That over in Leyton, Texas, there's a fellow named Jack Anderson who's been talking about a killing he did during a train robbery some twelve years ago.'

'Uh-huh.'

'Are you listening to me, Jim?'

'Yep. Fellow I never heard of called Anderson killed someone in a place I never heard of.'

'He didn't kill anyone in Leyton. That's where he lives now. He's a tough guy and he's trying hard to build a tougher reputation. He's talking about killing a Texas Ranger during a train robbery.'

'Uh-huh.'

'He's talking about your killing, Jim.'

'I never killed anyone.'

'You know what I mean. He's living the good life, too. A fellow by the name of Jack Anderson. You sure you don't know him?'

'No.'

'He wasn't part of your gang?'

'It wasn't my gang.'

'I just thought you should know. Maybe it was a different killing after all then.'

Jim Jackson stopped.

'What's he look like?'

'I don't know. I haven't seen him. I just heard that he's been living it up and talking loose. He even supposedly mentioned you by name. Gentleman Jim.'

Jim tried to focus on McRae's face. It was hard. The man's hat cast dark shadows over his face. There were two hats. They were moving left and right. Every so often they converged. Jim waited for such a convergence before he spoke.

'So why don't you arrest *him* and send *him* to hell, Mr Texas?'

'It's not that easy. You've already done time for that crime. No-one's interested in opening it up again.'

'I'm interested.'

'Which is why I told you.'

'You sure it's the same shooting?'

'Word is the fellow Anderson has been talking about how he gave up four members of the gang — the rest of the gang. You know what I'm saying. There were four of you jailed.'

'Was there?'

'You don't know?'

'Nope. The moment they — you — came for me I never heard about any of the others again.'

'Like I said, I thought you should know.'

Jim Jackson swayed slightly. There were too many thoughts criss-crossing his mind for him to be able to work through them all.

'I appreciate it,' he said. 'Maybe we should talk tomorrow.'

McRae smiled. 'Let's do that.'

'I think I might head home,' Jim said.

'I'm not sure I need any more whiskey.'

'You need me to walk you?'

'No, it's just here.'

'OK. Let's talk tomorrow.'

Jim took a couple of steps towards Rose's boarding house and then stopped. He turned. 'I never asked,' he said. 'What brings you to the Crossing?'

'My job,' McRae said. 'Like I said, I'm a bounty hunter now.'

4

Jim Jackson figured it was somewhere around nine o'clock when the two fellows he had tricked back at the mine in Santiago returned to town.

He was sitting on the plank walk outside Rose's front door, his feet splayed out on the dirt road, and a fourth cup of strong coffee in his hands. Amos was above him, leaning on the railing that ran alongside the outside edge of the plank walk. It never ceased to amaze Jim how much Amos could pick up through his senses of hearing and smell and touch.

'Blue Garner's not happy,' Amos said, even before the two riders came into Jim's sight.

Jim had been thinking about how he should have left town. The fact that he hadn't left the Crossing puzzled him. Maybe, he thought, it was a sub-conscious decision. Or maybe it was just that he'd

76

been drinking most of yesterday after-noon and evening. Also, he'd been pondering on a half-remembered conversation with Sam McRae, the Ranger who had brought an end to Jim's train robbing days. There had been something about a fellow fram-ing Jim for murder and that was why Jim had ended up doing all the hard time. A man — a *real* man — would be going in search of that fellow.

He'd also been trying to make sense of the fact that over in the Domino, folks were talking about a group of fellers who had set themselves up in the Bridge Hotel and were demanding money from businesses around town, and when Jim had been over in the Bridge Hotel there had indeed been a group of men that looked, well, suspicious. It meant nothing of course. The Domino was full of suspicious characters, too. But the sheriff, he'd been there in the Bridge Hotel, too, and he'd looked angry with those men. Another snatch of half-remembered conversation flitted across his mind, he couldn't recall from where. 'I told you there was trouble in town.'

'Spitting blood,' Amos said.

Jim Jackson stood up. His bones ached. 'You got hearing like an owl, Amos.'

Blue Garner and Henry Slade rode into sight.

'What did you do to them, Jim?' Amos asked. 'Blue's looking to kill you.'

Jim could hear Blue's words himself now. 'Where's that son of a bitch? I'm going to tear his head off.' All of a sudden it felt like there was a piece of lead the size of a fist wedged deep in Jim's gut.

Then Blue Garner simply shouted out, 'Junk! I'm coming for you. Jackson, get out here now and face me like a man!'

'Jim?' Amos said.

'They followed me yesterday. They were looking to rob me.' Jim could hear the tremble in his own voice.

'And?'

'I trapped them in the mine.' The

fist-sized obstruction in Jim's belly felt like it was expanding. He could taste bile in his throat.

'What mine?'

'Over at Bluegrass. I mean, Santiago.' His throat was dry. The words were little more than a croak.

'The old copper mine? That place was closed before I even got here.'

As the two riders got closer Jim could see how dirty they were. Their faces and hands were black and their clothes torn and dirtied. Blue Garner's hat was gone and his hair was wild. Even the whites of his eyes were dark with dirt.

'Junk!' he called again. 'Shaky!'

'Henry's quiet,' Amos said. 'A quiet Henry Slade is a dangerous Henry Slade.'

Main Street was already busy with people going about their morning business, there were horses tied up outside the store and along by the livery, wagons were being unloaded, and there was smoke and cooking in the air. But folks were stopping and looking and now more came outside to see what the fuss was about.

Jim Jackson could feel fear starting to bubble inside his belly as if the obstruction there had turned molten. He should have left town yesterday like he planned. He could have been long gone and never seen Blue and Henry again. He wondered if he should run now. He could slip back into Rose's, grab his stuff — even just the saddle bags of money — and be gone. There was still a chance.

Blue Garner saw him.

'Shaky!' he roared and pulled that Spencer rifle from its scabbard and he worked the action, raised the gun, and fired all in a single motion.

Jim had no idea where the bullet landed. The moment he saw Blue reaching for the gun he had crouched down, dragging Amos with him. He heard the lever being jacked again and there was another shot and this time he felt the whistle of the bullet and he heard it smash into the wood behind him.

'Told you he wasn't happy,' Amos said.

'Stand up, Shaky!' Blue Garner yelled. 'Get down here in the street.'

'Spilt hot coffee all over my pants,' Amos said.

Jim heard the action being worked a third time. He heard the rise of voices all around the street. A woman was saying, 'Oh my gosh,' and a dog was barking. He could hear his own heart beating as loud as if it was a blacksmith hammering on an anvil. He realized he had his eyes closed, but that aside he was crouched over Amos, trying to protect the blind man. It was probably the first brave thing he'd done in years.

He opened his eyes and looking between the wooden rails, he could see Blue Garner on the horse, rifle pointed towards him. Even through the dirt he could see Blue's face was bright red. His eyes were wide open and he was shaking with anger.

Jim Jackson stood up. At least that way Blue would be less likely to hit Amos.

'You son of a bitch,' Blue Garner said

and adjusted his aim slightly.

'Hold on there, Blue. Just hold on.'

Sheriff Wagner was striding towards Blue Garner. He had a revolver in his hand, although it was held low by his waist, and he wore no hat and only had his vest on over his bare, black-haired chest.

'Hold on,' he said again. 'You can't go around shooting folks. Not for no reason. Not in my town.'

Blue Garner's gaze never wavered from Jim Jackson. Any moment Jim Jackson expected that rifle bullet to knock him backwards into eternity. The thought was, in one way, quite enticing. In his peripheral vision Jim saw Amos struggling to his feet.

'Careful, Amos,' he said. 'There's liable to be bullets flying.'

Blue Garner looked across to the sheriff.

'It ain't for no reason, Sheriff.'

Jim Jackson became aware of more people coming out onto the street.

'He set us up,' Henry Slade said.

'Tried to kill us.'

The sheriff looked from Blue to Henry and back to Blue. Then he slowly turned and looked over to the plank walk outside Rose's boarding house where Jim Jackson stood next to Amos, who had a long wet coffee stain on his pants.

'Junk tried to kill you?'

'Trapped us in the mine,' Blue Garner said.

There was the sound of footsteps on wood and Jim Jackson realized Rose had stepped outside onto the boards next to him and Amos. He quickly looked at her and said, 'You should go inside, Rose. They want to shoot me.'

'Exactly why I'm standing next to you. Maybe they'll think twice.'

Rose was grey-haired and wore wire-framed round eye glasses. She had a blue apron over a long gingham dress. She'd come West with her husband and children some twenty years before. Her children were still alive but had long since headed over to San Francisco where they frequently wrote her to come, telling her it was a comfortable and civilized life and there was a home for her there where life would be a whole lot better than it was in the Crossing. Rose always said she intended to take them up on the offer when she was a little older, but for now she'd wait here just a little longer on the off-chance that her husband would one day come home.

Frankie Golde had headed north-west ten years before chasing gold. Rose said how Frankie had told her, 'With a name like ours it's written in the stars.' And he'd been right. He struck lucky and found a good seam and he sent money back and she was able to buy the boarding house and all the furnishings inside it and then, one day, she realized she hadn't heard from him in a while. She never heard from him again. Nevertheless, she would tell Jim and Amos how it simply wouldn't do for her not to be here when he finally came home.

'Trapped you in the mine?' Sheriff Wagner said.

'Brought a ton of rocks down on us.'

Sheriff Wagner cast another quick look over at Jim Jackson. He must have realized there was now a lady in line of sight because he quickly turned back to Blue and said, 'You lower that rifle now, son.'

Blue stared at him for a few more seconds. 'I'm going to kill him,' he said, lowering the rifle so it pointed to the ground.

'Thank you,' the sheriff said. 'Now, what in the hell are you talking about?'

'We were at the mine and he trapped us and we almost died.'

'What mine?'

Jim Jackson saw Henry Slade shaking his head at Blue Garner as if to say *enough was enough, just leave it*. But Blue was too riled up.

'Over in Santiago.'

'Santiago, for chrissakes? What in hell's name were you doing in Santiago?'

Now Blue must have realized that he might have said too much, might have

85

been leading himself down a track he didn't want to go down in front of just about everyone in town. The plank walks were packed and folks had stopped what they were doing, and everyone was watching and listening. One fellow who was loading a heavy box into the back of the wagon over by the mercantile was paused with that box in mid-air as if it weighed nothing.

'We were just riding around. We were looking for stuff to sell.'

'Really.'

'Shaky was over there.'

'Santiago?'

'Yeah. Don't know why.'

'And he trapped you in the mine?'

There were a few sniggers of laughter from the still growing audience.

'Yeah,' Blue Garner said, his face reddening further.

The sheriff turned towards Jim Jackson.

'Jim?'

'I've no idea what he's talking about,' Jim Jackson said.

'You son of a bitch!' Blue said, and started to raise his gun again.

'Blue!' the sheriff said.

'He's lying.'

'You weren't in Santiago? In the mine, Jim?' Wagner asked.

'No.'

Across the street Jim Jackson noticed Li'l Lil standing outside the Domino. She was alongside Sam McRae and the big bearded man was leaning down, whispering something to her. Just to the right of them he saw Little Joe Grubber, his head underneath that yellow hat, pushed forward as he watched and listened intently, full of interest. Jim saw the doc and Connery, and Mannie from the stables. He noticed a couple of the fellows — including the scar-faced man — from the Bridge Hotel had wandered up to see what the fuss was about, too. Behind them was Big Mingus grinning like this was the best show he'd seen since they last hanged someone in Parker's Crossing.

'Midday,' Blue said, addressing Jim

Jackson directly. 'You know what you did. You find yourself a gun and you come at midday and I'll shoot you dead for it.'

'There'll be no killing in my town,' Wagner said.

'You telling me a man can't call out a fair duel?' Blue asked.

A murmour of agreement riffled around the crowd. This was good entertainment. A gunfight at midday would be even better. And if Junk Jackson was the one to be wasted, well, what kind of waste was that?

'You can't call out a duel for no reason,' Wagner said. 'And a duel with . . . Jim. That's not a fair duel. That's as close to murder as you can get.'

'He should've thought of that before trapping me in the mine.'

Someone called out, 'Midday!'

Somebody else said, 'Sounds fair to me.'

A few people clapped and stamped their feet.

'It's like ancient Rome,' Jim Jackson

whispered to no-one but himself.

'You read too much,' Amos whispered back.

'No,' Wagner said to Blue Garner.

'Let 'em shoot it out!' a fellow called from outside the Domino. Jim Jackson saw Sam McRae look over at the fellow. Was Sam smiling?

More people called out, 'Midday!' and stamped their feet, too. Blue Garner was grinning now. A moment ago he'd been digging a hole of ridicule for himself, but now folks were back on his side. A man calling out a gunfight was a brave man, although had most of them stopped to think, they might have considered that calling out the local drunk who didn't even own a handgun mightn't really be so courageous after all.

'Midday,' Blue said, looking over at Jim. 'Right here.'

The sheriff looked over at Jim. 'I can outlaw it, Jim. Just say the word.'

A few people booed.

Jim looked across the street, at all

those people staring at him. Clearly, they didn't like him or think much of him. They all knew him as Junk or Shaky or Trembles. It was an easy out. They knew him as a coward. He could hide behind the sheriff's offer and no-one would feel any different towards him. Nothing would change. He was what he was. But . . . there was something else. It was the way Rose had come and stood alongside him, protecting him in her own simple way. It was the way McRae was smiling over there on the steps of the Domino. It was Little Joe Grubber who didn't know why Jim trembled so much. It was the way Li'l Lil always had a smile and a kind word and a soft touch and a look for him.

But it was also the way that he — that Jim Jackson — had grabbed Amos and pulled him down out of the line of Blue's fire, and crouched over the blind man, protecting him. That had been instinct. But it had felt good. It had opened a tiny door of something somewhere inside his mind.

He could do this. He could be brave again.

'Jim?' the sheriff said.

'Can I borrow your gun?' Jim asked.

'Mine?' Wagner said.

'I don't have one.' A ripple of laughter, some of it tinged with pity, ran round the crowd. Beside him, Jim heard Rose whisper, 'You don't have to do this, Jim,' and he felt her hand on his back.

Friends, he thought. They can give you all the courage you need.

'I guess so,' the sheriff said.

'Then midday it is,' Jim Jackson said, and a cheer went up around Parker's Crossing.

5

They walked back through Rose's boarding house and out into her yard where a few hens scattered from beneath their feet. Rose, or maybe one of her boarders before Jim had arrived, had put up a pinewood fence to keep the chickens from wandering too far. There was a gate in the fence, right back there by the outhouse, and through the gate was scrubland leading to some meadow grass and eventually a copse of trees that found enough moisture deep down to grow to a decent height.

'You really don't need to do this,' Rose said. If she'd said it once she said it ten times.

Jim Jackson strapped on the sheriff's gun belt as they walked towards the trees. He got it so the gun was lying just right on his thigh. It felt like there was a memory there, right in the thigh muscle. It had been ten, maybe twelve years, but it felt right, it felt a little like coming home.

'I do need to do it, Rose,' he said.

'But . . . ' Her words faltered.

'But I'm going to die?'

'No, I don't mean that.'

'You don't think I'm going to die?'

She was walking alongside him, still in her blue apron. Behind them Amos was holding onto Little Joe Grubber's tiny hand. Little Joe had come running across the street the moment the ultimatum had been issued.

'You gonna shoot Blue Garner dead, Shaky?' he'd asked breathlessly. There had been excitement in his eyes. Little Joe was, Jim Jackson thought, the only person in town who genuinely believed in him.

Now Jim Jackson cast a quick look back towards Amos and Joe. He smiled. Behind them he saw a few folks standing back at the edge of town watching the small group walk towards the trees. But none of them followed. To them Jim Jackson was Junk. Midday was only a couple of hours away. They'd no doubt see all they'd need to see then.

'I . . . I just don't know,' Rose said.

Jim Jackson tightened the gun belt. There, that was just right. He'd tie it down when he stopped over there in the trees.

'Have faith,' Jim said.

'At least you ain't cold,' Little Joe said from behind. 'Leastways, you ain't shaking.'

For the first half an hour he didn't fire a bullet. He simply stood in the shade of the trees, away from the prying eyes of everyone in town, and practiced drawing that gun from the holster. The first few times he got it wrong. He wasn't pulling it far enough. Just a fraction of inch but it was enough. The holster was different from the one he'd had back in the day. A couple of times he even dropped the gun. He heard Rose cry quietly in despair on those occasions but he told her not to worry. He readjusted the belt and he recalibrated his mind and within thirty minutes he was pulling that gun smoothly from the holster. His arm, though, was hurting. He knew he was going to have to take it easy. He didn't want to tire out muscles that hadn't been used in an age.

Amos, sitting on a stump where someone had cut down a tree for lumber or firewood, said aloud to anyone who was listening, 'He sounds pretty smooth to me. Never knew he could do that.'

From behind, Sam McRae said, 'You never knew?'

Jim, Rose, Little Joe and Amos turned towards to the new arrival.

'Who's that?' Amos said. Then he sniffed the air and said, 'Lil, too, if I'm not mistaken.'

'I'll take that as a compliment,' Li'l Lil said. 'On account of I've bathed and perfumed this morning.'

'Sam McRae,' Jim said. 'Sam's a bounty hunter.'

'An old acquaintance of Jim's,' Sam said.

'He's the one who caught me,' Jim said, pulling the sheriff's gun from its holster in a smooth and quick movement that made Li'l Lil's eyes widen. This time Jim pulled the trigger and the bullet smashed into a tree twenty feet away. The shot sounded awfully loud in the warm still morning.

'*Caught* you?' Rose said.

'Were you falling?' Little Joe asked.

Jim put the gun back in his holster. He rolled his shoulders, relaxing the muscles. Then he drew and fired and this time the movement was just a blur to those watching and two bullets smashed into the same tree.

'That'll give them something to think about in town,' Amos said, grinning beneath his bandaged eyes.

'Wow,' Little Joe Grubber said.

'What did he catch you doing?' Rose said.

'Gentleman Jim Jackson was a train robber,' Sam McRae said. 'Back in Texas.'

96

'A train robber?'

'A gentleman,' Jim said, drawing and firing once more. This time three shots that sounded as close together as the sounds from a rattlesnake's tail.

'I don't believe he ever shot anyone,' McRae said. 'He most definitely never killed anyone. But there was no doubting he was the quickest gunman I ever saw in Texas.'

★   ★   ★

Blue Garner was drunk.

He came out of the Domino and steadied himself against the door frame before stepping out of the shadows, off the plank walk, and into the fierce sunlight. Behind him came Henry Slade and then a whole posse of cowboys and tradesmen, gamblers and drinkers, and Connery and the Domino girls. On both sides of the main street people were emerging from their buildings and lining the plank walks. Mannie was walking up from the livery, and there was the crowd from the

Bridge Hotel, too, with Scarface looking cool, almost sinister, in a black coat in the midday sun.

Jim Jackson stepped out from Rose's boarding house, and behind came his own small band of supporters: Rose and Amos and Little Joe Grubber and Li'l Lil and Sam McRae. Ghost, and a couple of Little Joe's other business boys, came running over as soon as they saw him and Joe whispered to them, 'I ain't never seen anyone shoot so fast as Shaky. He was the fastest gun in Texas.'

The sheriff came out of his office and wandered into the street. He watched Jim step down from the shade in front of Rose's house.

'There's still time, Jim,' he said. 'Nobody's gonna look down upon you.'

'Any more than they already do,' someone said and a lot of people laughed.

Jim walked out to the middle of the street.

'I'm ready,' he said. He could feel the heat of the sun burning through his clothes. There was a knot of fear in his belly, but he'd lived so long with that feeling that it was no different to any other day from the last ten years. In fact, it felt good. It felt *better*. Something had happened these last few days. A few people had believed in him. Perhaps he had even begun to believe in himself.

He watched Blue Garner swaying slightly as he made his own way forwards.

'You need me to come a bit closer, Blue?' Jim Jackson said, and a few people laughed and while others exclaimed 'ohhh' as if to say *Blue won't like that.*

'You shouldn't have done it, Shaky. You shouldn't have shut me in the dark like that.'

Sheriff Wagner said, 'You boys ready?'

They both nodded.

'You know the rules. There's no pacing. I'm going to count down from three. That's all. Jim?'

'Yes.'

'Blue?'

'Get on with it.'

Wagner looked left and right. Jim figured he was checking that there was no-one behind either duellist.

'OK,' Wagner said. For a moment his eyes caught Jim's. There was an expression of sorrow on the sheriff's face. He seemed to be saying, *I'm sorry it had to come to this, Jim*. Then he looked at Blue Garner and said, 'Three.'

A silence came over Parker's Crossing.

'Two.'

Now a stillness. As still as an August day when the wind stopped and it felt like it would never be cool and comfortable again.

'One.'

Blue Garner was grinning as he went for his gun. It was a grin that told all watching how much he was enjoying this. Not a lot of folks got the chance to have a gunfight with a drunken mess of a man like Shaky Jackson. It was a gunfight you couldn't lose. You could live a lot on the fact that you'd had a gunfight, a real live stand-up-in-the-street gunfight. You'd tell your friends and you'd tell strangers and if you ever had kids you'd tell them, and you'd tell *their* kids, and although this land stretched on forever there really wasn't that many people who'd actually had a gunfight, not a goddamn real-to-goodness shoot-out in the street gunfight and you could get a lot of drinks bought for you for a long time on the fact that you were one of the few who'd been in one.

And in Blue's slightly unfocussed eyes, there seemed to be a message to all that he was saying *I bet you wished you'd thought of it, that you'd thought of challenging Shaky Jackson to a duel.*

Blue Garner's handgun never even cleared his holster.

Most folks said later that they didn't actually see what had happened because they were watching Blue rather than Jim Jackson. But even before Blue's gun was clear of his holster there were three shots, three explosions, three deadly echoes cascading across Main Street and all three bullets took Blue Garner in the chest (one right in the heart, the doc said later) and knocked him backwards off his feet.

The silence beyond those gunshots and the stillness didn't break for about five seconds.

It was a silence and stillness of disbelief and then somebody said, 'Son of a gun' and then Henry Slade stepped forward from the crowd and looked at Shaky who was still standing in the street, the sheriff's gun smoking in his hand, and he shook his head quietly in amazement. Now someone rushed forward and leaned over Blue's body and they declared the man dead. And then the silence broke as people started to talk. It was the talk of amazement, of witnessing something incredible and unbelievable.

Amongst it all Jim Jackson was trembling like he'd never trembled before. It wasn't fear. It wasn't relief. He had a killed a man. He'd never had to do that before and it felt awful, terrible. It felt like right now God was looking down upon him from that endless blue sky and cutting all ties and bonds.

'What alternative did I have?' Jim Jackson said, speaking to God.

'None at all, son,' the sheriff said. 'But where in the hell did you learn to shoot like that?'

Jim looked at him. For a moment he felt puzzled as if he couldn't work out why he was standing in this street and all these people were rushing towards him, smiling, speaking, and reaching out to touch him. Amongst it all he slipped the sheriff's gun back into its holster, and he undid the tie and the belt and he handed it back to Sheriff Wagner.

'I guess we can't call you Junk any longer,' somebody said. 'Come on. Let me be the first to buy you a drink.'

6

That night, for the first time ever, Jim Jackson found himself sleeping all night in a small room upstairs in the Domino, the window open and the warm air and the night sounds drifting in over him, and Li'l Lil asleep up against him.

It had been a betrayal, of course. A betrayal against Jennifer Anne, the woman he loved. The woman for whom he had first ventured West. A woman who almost certainly never thought of him any more, probably didn't even remember him, and was most likely married now anyway.

Nevertheless, to Jim Jackson, it was a betrayal against an ideal that had been there all along and had maybe carried him through his darkest times.

But what was such a betrayal against the fact that today he had killed a man?

People had bought him drinks, slapped him on the back and told him they knew that inside he had courage. Some folks told him that Blue Garner was no good and had it coming. Most wanted to know where he learned to shoot like that and how many folks had he killed before.

And it had gone on all day. Sometime around dusk the drink had stopped touching him. He was drunk, but it was a different drunk. A good drunk, maybe? Or perhaps just killing a man wasn't the sort of thing that God allowed a man to hide from with whiskey. Later on Amy had played the piano and the Domino had been a good place for once, for Jim Jackson.

When they were in bed he recalled telling Lil something about Jennifer Anne and Lil putting a soft finger on his lips, her green eyes and roughly cut corn-coloured hair soft in the light of a candle, saying, 'It doesn't matter, it's a different world.'

He'd been twenty-three years old and

Jennifer Anne was twenty-one. The prettiest girl in Clark County, Illinois. Her father was Hubert Hodgeson, the richest man in Clark County. Maybe the richest man in the five counties area. Back then, Hubert had made one thing absolutely clear. James Jackson was not good enough for Jennifer Anne. Wasn't good enough then, and never would be.

Jim Jackson had said to Jennifer Anne, 'Give me a year. Just one year.'

He told her he'd be back, rich enough, and with enough style to change Hubert's mind. Jennifer Anne said she didn't want him to go. She told him she loved him just as he was. She wasn't worried about money or manners. 'Well,' she'd said, 'I like a man with manners and your manners are fine, James Jackson.'

'Not as far as your father is concerned,' he told her.

'I don't care. We can do what we want. I'm twenty-one years old.'

'You're a tightly knit family,' he said.

'You, your brother, your parents. I don't want to break that up. And you wouldn't be happy. You'd come to resent me.'

'No, I wouldn't.'

The conversation had taken place on the corner of Second Avenue and First Street, Chapeltown, Clark County. Behind them, one of Hubert's huge shops cast an imposing shadow over the street.

'Yes, you would. And I'm not going to risk it.'

People walking by in the late afternoon sunshine smiled at them. Some said hello to Jennifer Anne, knowing she was the daughter of one of the town's most influential men.

So Jim Jackson headed West, because it was West where fortunes were being made. He took a small case of clothes which he topped up with novels and engineering books because he enjoyed reading and one day he planned to be an engineer. Gentleman Jim Jackson was off to make a fortune so he could marry the girl he loved.

He didn't recall how much of this he told Li'l Lil, lying there in the moonlight, his head numb but not hurting, his heart too. Lil had run a finger over the multitude of whipping scars on his back and legs and she had cried a little over them. Maybe he told her all of it. But in the end it didn't matter. He'd killed a man and he'd made love to a girl who wasn't Jennifer Anne and he was no longer, at least for a day, Junk Jackson.

In the morning perhaps the whole world would be different.

In the morning they found Sam McRae's body hanging by his ankles from the river bridge.

It was Little Joe Grubber who found McRae's body. He had gone down to the river with two buckets for the livery. He was kneeling down on the gravel when he glanced to his left and saw the body hanging from the wooden bridge.

The bridge was low. Prior to it being constructed one could still cross the river on horseback by careful fording, especially if the rains had been rare which was most of the time, but the water was gradually eroding the banks and the drop from trail to riverbed eventually got too much for wagons. The lowness of the bridge meant that McRae's chest and head were in the water.

Little Joe spent a few moments looking at the body from a distance, then he carefully placed his two half-filled buckets on the ground and ran over for a closer look. He knew a dead man when he saw one. He'd seen Southee Bell and he'd seen Blue Garner. And now he saw Sam McCrae who only yesterday he'd been talking with in the trees back of Rose Golde's boarding house. Once he knew for sure that McRae was beyond help he ran into town and started hammering on the sheriff's door.

It turned out that McRae's throat had been cut. When the sheriff and the doc and a couple of helpers heaved

Sam McRae's body up out of the water, his head lolled back and his throat opened as if he had a second mouth.

Jim Jackson was there, standing at the water's edge in the crowd. Li'l Lil was holding his hand. They, along with a couple of dozen other folks, had heard Joe Grubber banging on the sheriff's door and shouting there was a dead man in the river. Sam McRae was about the last person in town who Jim Jackson thought would be murdered. The man had been big, he'd been tough. He'd given off an aura of confidence and ability. Hell, he'd been a Texas Ranger. Jim Jackson shivered in the early morning coolness and Lil squeezed his hand as he watched them laying Sam McRae down on the bridge.

'He was talking to me yesterday,' Lil said. 'Before your . . . your gunfight.' She spoke quietly. They were standing at the edge of the crowd. It was the type of gathering where no matter how many people were there, you felt and stood alone. A man with his throat cut hanging from a bridge will do that to you, Jim thought.

'I saw you.'

'He said you were a fine man. I was worried you were about to die, but he said, 'Don't worry. Jim's a fine man. He's a better man than people know'.'

Someone brought a flatbed cart up onto the bridge, drawn by a mule that looked like it had a skin complaint, its left flank was raw and pink.

'He tried to apologize to me,' Jim said. 'I was drunk and not very gracious. But then I thought why should I have been gracious? He was the one who put me away in hell.'

'He seemed like a good man.'

'He was a good man.'

There were dozens of flies settling on the mule's flank. It tried to flick its tail at them but the majority of the insects were out of reach.

'But he deserved better than this.' Jim Jackson couldn't help but wonder what had happened. Who had done this, and how had they managed it?

Lil said, 'He told me there was some trouble in town — I mean, we all know there's trouble in town, don't we — but that he was going to sort it. I think he meant . . . You know, Southee Bell. And Connery told me some men have been demanding money though he was refusing to give in to them. There's others, too. I was . . . pleased. He — Sam — seemed to be sure of himself. He said he'd been following a trail of trouble and it was time to end it.'

They were loading McRae onto the flatbed now.

'Rose, too. Apparently,' Jim said.

Lil looked at him. She was about three inches shorter than he and her eyes, looking up, had a softness and a purity to them that he'd never noticed before. He wanted to kiss her. He wanted to do something right by her. But despite what had happened yesterday he could already feel the old Jim Jackson sneaking back. He wanted a drink. He wanted to hide in a bottle, maybe toast McRae on his journey to hell. Yesterday was starting to feel like a dream.

'Rose?'

'Amos said someone is demanding money off her, too.'

'She's just a landlady.'

'Uh-huh.'

'Who is it, Jim? Who's behind it?'

Jim thought of Amos saying if he knew he'd tell Sheriff Wagner and the sheriff could arrest the men. He recalled the conversations in the Domino two nights back when folks pretty much named those Bridge Hotel fellows as the ones, and he pictured the sheriff standing up to them in the Bridge Hotel. He heard McRae saying he was a bounty hunter and he saw all those fellows in the Bridge Hotel staring at McRae.

He thought of Amos saying that if he could still see he'd probably try and help Rose.

'I think I need to speak to Rose,' Jim said.

Over at the bridge the doc and the

sheriff were walking behind that flatbed wagon as the mule slowly pulled Sam McRae back into Parker's Crossing. Folks turned and started following them and Jim Jackson heard Little Joe Grubber call out, 'Don't forget your water! Upstream of the bridge water only! No blood in Joe Grubber's water!'

★   ★   ★

Rose said, 'It was a youngish fellow. Polite. No, he didn't have a scar. He stopped me in the street — I was coming back from the Mercantile with some flour, milk powder, and a salted ham. All you boys sure like to eat, don't you?'

Aside from Jim and Amos, Rose also boarded Freeman Grainger, who was albino, only twenty-two, and was working for Father Thornley over at the church, but the church didn't have anywhere to house him yet.

'What did he say?' Jim asked.

'He asked me if I was the good lady

who ran the boarding house just along from the Domino. I told him I was, and asked him who he was. He said it didn't matter, but because I was a lady and he was trying to help me and I'd probably want to get in touch with him again, I should call him Luke. 'Luke what?' I asked. I think he plucked a name out of thin air — Luke Hamilton — because he wanted to come across as nice and helpful. And to be honest, he did appear that way to start with.

'He asked me my name and then he said, 'Rose, there's talk of trouble coming.' 'What kind of trouble?' I said. I think I might have asked if the Apache were coming back. He shook his head and said, 'No, there's talk of some folks heading into the Crossing who just want to cause . . . trouble. Bad trouble.' I told him he should talk to Sheriff Wagner. He said he'd do that, but that the sheriff was just one man. I said, 'What about Julio Ramez?' and he said, 'Yes, two men then. But Rose, they can't protect everyone.' 'What do you mean protect?' I asked. He said it — this trouble, I assume — was coming across the state, coming from Texas, from the East. That people with businesses were the target. I told him I didn't have a business, I had a boarding house. He shrugged and said, 'Your boarders pay you, no?' And I think then was when I saw the niceness in his eyes replaced by something else. Something hard. I asked him what he was selling, why he had stopped me in the street — except then I realized we weren't in the street — I had come round the back and there was no-one there but him and me. He was wearing a coat and he opened it and he had a gun and he said he was a good man, a good man with a gun, and for just a small payment he would look after me.'

'Two dollars a day,' Amos said.

'You knew all of this?' Jim Jackson said.

'I told you a couple of days back,' Amos said.

They were in Rose's kitchen. The

116

smell of pastry cooking made Jim Jackson feel hungry. Through the window they could see the chickens in Rose's yard.

'You live in your own world — or have up until now,' Rose said, and Jim Jackson felt knives twisting in his heart once more. It was, he thought, time to pull those knives out once and for all. If he couldn't do it on the back of what had happened yesterday then he'd never be able to do it.

'Did you tell Wagner?' Jim asked.

'Tell him what? Someone offered to be my friend? This man — Luke Hamilton — wasn't threatening me. Not really, though it felt a little like it. I asked him what would happen if I said no, thank you. He shrugged, and said, 'Maybe nothing'.'

'You didn't agree to pay him?'

'I said I'd think about and he said he'd come and see me again.'

'And has he?'

'No.'

'Not yet,' Amos added. 'But now

Southee Bell and that new fellow Sam McRae have both been found dead, I reckon it won't be long. They were messages loud and clear, if you want my opinion.'

'And what should I say when he does come back?' Rose asked. 'I don't have fourteen dollars a week to give him, or anyone. I give a dollar to Father Thornley on a Sunday. You think maybe God will protect me?'

7

Jim Jackson said to Sheriff Wagner, 'I want Sam McRae's gun.'

Wagner said, 'Jim, what happened yesterday. I think I — all of us — under-estimated you.'

'Under-estimated? I'm not sure that's how I would describe the way you've all treated me.'

'No, you're right. I'm sorry. I apologize.'

'On behalf of your town?'

Wagner pulled a puzzled expression. 'No, just on behalf of myself.'

'Sorry, I'm being obtuse.'

'Obtuse,' Wagner said, as if he'd never heard the word.

'Just two nights ago, Sam McRae apologized to me, too. But he apologized on behalf of all of Texas.'

'For what?'

'For sending me to hell. You know my story?'

'I've heard some rumours. I try not to pay too much attention to rumours. I was going to come and find you yesterday. Just to talk. But you were — you were something of a hero.'

'For killing a man?'

'For standing up to a man.'

They were in Wagner's office. The sheriff had poured them both a strong black coffee and he was hunched over his wooden desk rolling a cigarette. Behind him, pinned to the wall were a couple of faded wanted posters with the corners curling. There was a stove in the corner that gave off too much heat but was needed for the coffee. 'It's a compromise,' Wagner had said about the stove whilst making the coffee. A bucket of Joe Grubber's blood-free river water stood next to the stove and there were rifles and shotguns in a rack on the wall with a padlocked silver chain running through all the trigger guards. A door in the back of the room led to stairs, at the top of which were two cells. Jim Jackson had spent a drunken night in one of those cells once. The room — and the sheriff — always smelled sweet. The morning after that drunken night Jim had asked the sheriff what the smell was, said it had been making him nauseous all night. 'Bay Rum tonic,' the sheriff had said. 'I get it mailed in from St Louis.' Wagner had then sniffed the air and said, 'If you don't always get the time or inclination to wash, Junk, then perhaps you should get some, too.'

'Did you really trap Henry and Blue in the mine?' Wagner asked now.

'They trapped themselves. It's not a place to go unless you know your way around.'

The sheriff shook his head and smiled. He passed the made cigarette to Jim and started working on another.

Wagner said, 'You were very fast with my gun.'

'I never set out to be fast. Some folks can run fast. Some can jump high and I've met a few who can talk several languages. I just ... it was just

121

something I could do.'

'You were a gunfighter?'

Jim paused, then said, 'Train robber.'

Wagner looked up from working on the cigarette. His face was weathered from years in the New Mexico sun and his hair was bleached a light brown. There were lines around his eyes, and the left eye was pulled down very slightly as if once the skin there had been cut and the wound had healed tight.

'McRae was the one caught you?'

'Uh-huh.'

'So you've done your time.'

'And then some. If you want to know, I never killed anyone, well not until yesterday — although they said I did. You want to know a funny thing?'

'Go on,' Wagner said.

'On the day McRae arrested me — he and another Ranger — I was packed up and ready to go home. I'd only come West to make a quick fortune so I could marry my sweetheart. I was going to find gold, but that wasn't as easy as the newspaper stories made out. One time I was bemoaning this fact to a stranger in a saloon in Kansas City as I worked my way home, pretty much convinced I'd worsened rather than bettered my position with the girl in question, when the fellow suggested I might want to ride with him for a while. Four weeks later a bunch of us hauled some logs across a track down in Texas and when that train stopped, we simply walked through the carriages and . . . well, we probably made more money that day than most folk up in the gold rush territories do in a year. I didn't even have to fire a shot — although on other occasions there was a guard or a passenger who figured themselves a hero. Usually a quick draw and placing a bullet square in the carriage clock was enough to convince them that heroics weren't wise.

'So that's what I did, and I'm not proud of it, but I never shot or hurt anyone and I let the women keep their rings and on the day that McRae came for me, I was packed and ready to go home to Jennifer Anne.'

Wagner flicked a Lucifer into life, leant forwards and lit Jim's cigarette, then his own. He lifted his booted feet — no spurs — up onto the table. He smoked his cigarette and drank some coffee. Jim had smoked a pipe way back in Illinois, and he had smoked cigarettes whilst in Hans Freidlich's train robbing gang. But ten years in the convict leasing system had cured him of the habit. Now he coughed a little when he smoked.

After a while Wagner said, 'Jim, you can't just walk in here and start asking for a dead man's possessions. Why do you want McRae's gun?'

'I don't have one.'

'Buy one. There's a couple of Colts at Mulligan's store. You've got to ask for them.'

'I don't want to buy one.'

'You've got enough money.'

Wagner's eyes locked onto Jim's.

'Is there an unspoken question

there?' Jim asked.

'Nope.' Sheriff Wagner hauled his feet off the desk and stood up. 'You want more coffee?' He appeared stiff when he first moved after sitting for a while.

'Yes, thank you.' Jim held out his cup. He noticed that the sheriff limped very slightly as he walked, too. It wasn't something that he had ever observed before. This close up, the sheriff looked a little old for the job.

As he poured two more cups of coffee Wagner said, 'Folks know you got money. It was only a matter of time before someone tried to take it off you. Wouldn't surprise me if there ain't a couple of folks right now scrabbling around up at Santiago trying to find it.'

Jim thought of the money back in his room at Rose's in his saddle bags. Once in Illinois, in that other life, he'd read a story by a writer called Poe. The story was about a letter that everyone was desperately searching for, although Jim couldn't remember why. All the characters in the tale were convinced that the letter would by necessity be hidden in an elaborate and secure hiding place — so the perpetrator had simply done the opposite and hidden it in plain sight. It might work for a few days, but he knew sooner or later he was going to have to move that money again.

'I hope they're careful,' Jim said. 'Those mines can be a death trap if you don't know your way around.'

Wagner handed him the refreshed cup. 'My point is you could buy a gun. Mulligan would be happy with the business, too.'

The way Wagner said that caused a connection in Jim's mind.

'He's not got some extra expenses right now, has he?'

Wagner sat down. He grunted and sighed. 'Damn bones.' Then he looked at Jim Jackson and said, 'Extra expenses?'

Jim said, 'Southee Bell supposedly had extra expenses that he refused to pay.'

Wagner picked up his cigarette from his desk where it had been burning a mark on the wood. He took a long pull and blew smoke out towards the ceiling. He raised his cup to his mouth and drank equally long from the steaming cup.

'You know what, Jim, I can't believe I'm having this conversation with you. Of all people. Yesterday, or rather up until yesterday, you were just . . . well, you know.'

'Drunk.'

'Yes, I guess so. You were just . . . background. I don't mean that nastily. I paid you no more attention than I would the water troughs in the square or the sacks of feed piled up outside the livery. What happened?'

'I killed a man.'

'That's it?'

'Isn't that enough?'

'I guess so. I guess killing someone could change a man.'

'Rose — my landlady — she's been approached, too. Same as Southee Bell was.'

Wagner shook his head disbelievingly.

'Rose, too. Sons of bitches.'

'So . . . Mulligan?'

'Yep.'

'Others?'

'Yeah, I've had a few complaints. I think it's just starting.'

'You know who it is? I saw you standing up to some fellow in the Bridge a few nights back.'

'I'm pretty sure it's him. But, you know, no-one's done anything wrong. That fellow, and his cohort, they were laughing at me when they said it, but they said they'd heard the same thing I'd heard and they'd been offering to protect people for a small fee on account of I didn't seem able to.'

'If you're worried about the fact that McCrae's gun should be shipped home to his family then — '

'I don't think anyone's going to ship anything home. There's nothing on his person or in his room back at the Domino to suggest where home might be.'

'He would want me to have it. I

guarantee you that. I'll buy some bullets off Mulligan.'

'OK, you can have the gun. But . . . '

'But what?'

'Why do you want it?'

'In a funny way I feel like I owe it to McRae. Revenge, I mean. But really that's not it. They're threatening my landlady. Someone's got to stand up to them. There's only one of you, two with Julio — '

'Julio's off to Paradise on account of they had something similar to this last year.'

'Really? What did they do?'

'That's what Julio's gone to find out.'

'Then there's only one of you,' Jim said. 'Two of us.'

The sheriff picked up his cigarette again, but it burned his finger and he dropped it and then stamped on it.

'You don't think I'm up to it on my own?'

'I never said that.'

'It's OK. You want I should give you a badge?'

'No, thank you . . . although it might be a plan sometime.'

The sheriff smiled. 'Well, any help is welcome. But I'm not sure what we can do unless we catch one of 'em in the act. And I don't even know what act that would be.'

'Then I guess that's what we should do.'

'Catch 'em in the act? And how do you propose we do that?'

Jim Jackson said, 'Why are they doing this in the first place?'

'Money, I guess.'

'And what have I got?'

The sheriff had his makings out again. He was rolling a new cigarette without even looking at his fingers.

'Money,' he said.

'Then let's show them it,' Jim Jackson said. He held up his coffee mug and Sheriff Wagner touched his cup against it.

The sheriff opened a drawer in his desk and pulled out a bottle of what looked like good whiskey.

'Fancy a drink?'

'No, thank you,' Jim Jackson said. 'Those days are done.'

8

Jim Jackson sat on his horse just inside the tree line looking down upon Santiago again, at all that blue grass, and those deserted buildings. He thought about the sheriff reckoning there'd be folks in Santiago looking for his money and so Jim sat still for many minutes. There were birds down there but that was it. No other movement, no horses tied up outside the mine, or outside of anywhere. But still he sat. Up there in trees it was possible to get a comprehensive view of the old settlement, to see the line of the old roads and trails, to see which buildings still looked solid and had roofs, to see where a man might hide or run.

Jim and Wagner agreed they needed to show off the money and wait and see if these fellows made a move. But that alone was nothing. A plan was still needed. He'd discussed it with Amos. The two of them in his room back at Rose's boarding house. He'd told Amos about his visit with the sheriff and how now it was time for him to do something for Rose, and even for Sam McRae.

'But what do I do?' he asked. 'I need to draw 'em out of cover so that Wagner can arrest them legally.'

'Ain't gonna happen,' Amos said. He had a clean damp bandage over his eyes. Rose washed and boiled the bandages for him, and Amos always said it was one of his chief pleasures in life when it was the day for a clean one.

'Which bit?'

'Wagner's bit. Him, arresting them. How do you two figure that's going to go down?'

Jim Jackson was silent, thinking.

'The way Rose told it,' Amos went on, 'they're doing nothing wrong. They're just offering to help. Wagner can't arrest anyone for that.'

'Sooner or later they have to back up

those veiled threats.'

'Yes, they do. But they get to pick the time and place. They see anyone around, especially Wagner or probably any fellow who might have a gun — like you do now — they'll simply leave it. They don't seem in any hurry.'

'Time and place,' Jim Jackson said, thinking about those words.

'You know how they blindsided Sam McRae?' Amos asked.

Jim Jackson looked at his friend. 'No. What happened?'

'That's my point. No-one knows. Nobody in town heard or saw. And Sam was a big strong man according to Little Joe Grubber. They picked their time and place, Jim.'

Jim's mind was still racing.

'Say we had a time and place . . . ?'

'Then you've still got a problem. Wagner draws his gun and says hands up. What are they gonna do?'

'Kill him, I guess.'

'Yep.'

The two men were quiet for a while.

Amos said, 'And if you're there, too, they'll kill you as well. I know you're pretty fast. All of the Crossing is still talking about it. But how many of them did you say were in the Bridge Hotel?'

'If that's them.'

'That's what folks are saying. How many?'

'Four. Maybe five, if the fellow outside was part of it.'

'So you and Wagner are dead. Maybe one or two of them. And the rest carry on.'

'So the plan doesn't work.'

'Not *that* plan, not having Wagner arrest them like that.'

'We can't just shoot them.'

'Why not? They killed Southee — and by all reports he died hard — and they killed McRae. They're killers. Why not kill them?'

'Are you serious?'

'Maybe I'm just playing Devil's advocate. You know, I'd never heard of one of them — Devil's advocate — until you came to town.'

'Glad I was good for something.'

'You're good for a lot of things. Especially helping an old blind man.' Amos paused, cocked his head to one side as if thinking or remembering and said, 'You know, if I had seen those Apache coming and I had known what they were going to do, I'd have shot every one of them. Hell, if I had known in advance I'd have gone out and shot every one of 'em in the back whilst they were sleeping. Wouldn't have hesitated one single second. You'd have done the same, too, Jim.'

'That's different.'

'How is it different?'

'I . . . Look, we don't have that gift of foresight. We're civilized. *That's* what makes us different.'

'They were civilized, too. The Apache. But they were happy to do this to me . . .' Amos started undoing the bandage from around his head. 'And they killed my family. And I wish to God I had killed them first.'

Amos pulled off the bandage and

looked at Jim. His eyes were cloudy. Their surface was rippled and dry, like a peach or an apple that had been outside all day. The skin around the eyes, where the bandages protected it from the sun, was pale.

'You think Sam McRae's wife — if he had one — would have thought twice about shooting those fellows in their sleep if she had the chance and she knew what was going to happen?'

Amos lifted a hand and moved it back and forth in front of his eyes.

'Goddamn,' he said. 'Nothing.' He started wrapping the damp bandage around his eyes again.

'So we kill them,' Jim Jackson said, his tone simplistic.

'Devil's advocate,' Amos said. 'But if you knew who they were for sure, and you had the chance . . . '

'I'm not sure I could.'

'Then give me the gun and point my arm in the right direction.'

Jim smiled. 'Would that be any different?'

Amos said, 'See that's what I like about you, Jim Jackson. A man can have a good conversation. Most folks wouldn't even have considered that aspect of the situation.'

'I'm not a killer.'

'You killed — '

'Blue Garner. Yes, I know. And I still feel sick and I still struggle with it.'

'But when it was you or him, you did it.'

'Shooting four or five people just because they *might* do something is a little different.'

'Look at it differently, Jim. If you caught 'em in the act of killing someone, or threatening someone, and they didn't surrender to Wagner and they got shot — probably just before they shot you — would that be acceptable to your morals?'

'Maybe. But like you said, there's five of them, and even if we got one . . . '

'Then that's because you're still figuring on them choosing the time and place. How did you stop trains?'

'We'd lay a bunch of logs across the track.'

'Anywhere on the track?'

'How do you mean?'

'I mean on a piece of track in the centre of town, right by the station?'

'Of course not. Usually on a grade. Somewhere where we could hide. Somewhere where we could retreat quickly and get lost in the hills.'

'You choose the time and place and methodology?'

'Uh-huh.'

'And you were usually outnumbered, too?'

'Yep.'

'But it still came out in your favour?'

'Until McRae came along.'

'There you go then. Time and place.'

That had been earlier back at Rose's. Now, sitting there in the tree line Jim Jackson pulled a small leather pouch out of his pocket and started rolling a cigarette. Now that his hands didn't shake so much, smoking didn't seem such a bad habit to get back into. He'd bought the pouch, the tobacco, and a box of matches from Mulligan's. He'd bought a good knife and another gun too, despite having McRae's Colt on his hip. He didn't really have a plan yet, but he was trying to think ahead, trying to figure out the various ways things might go down. Back at Rose's he had a couple of dime Western pamphlets — Ned Buntline and Ed Wheeler — and though neither could hold a candle to Poe or Defoe they were enjoyable enough — and in one of them the hero, who was cornered by several outlaws who had taken his gun, still came out on top by dint of a hidden pistol in his boot-top. Jim had never figured out how one could hide a whole pistol in one's boot top but the idea of a hidden gun wasn't a bad one. That and setting up a few more surprises like the one he'd rigged in the mine. So he smoked his cigarette and he watched and he thought, and when his cigarette was finished he rode down into the abandoned town to lay some logs across the tracks.

* * *

Jim Jackson was in Santiago for the rest of the day and most of the next. He watered his horse from the well and fed her from a bag of feed he'd brought with him. He ate dried meat and wild onions and he slept in a room upstairs in what had been a hardware store. He re-hid his money and he gathered some of the tools from the mine and with the digging and cutting he was doing, he tore and dirtied his clothes.

And he got used to the feel of a six-gun resting on his hip once again.

When he came back to Parker's Crossing, aside from the stuff he'd already bought at Mulligan's, he'd bought a new coat, Levis, and a shirt from Vincent Quintana who sold clothes from a store not far along from the Bridge Hotel. He had a shave and a haircut at Jacque Bernard's barber shop, spent some time at the stage office talking prices and times and he hinted to the clerk that he might be thinking of moving on, and

141

then he purchased steaks and carrots from the mercantile that he brought back to Rose's.

By the time he, Amos, Rose, and Freeman Grainger sat down to eat those steaks in the early evening, Amos said the whole town was talking about Jim Jackson and his spending.

'And that's just what I hear,' Amos said. 'I'm sure if I had eyes then I'd see people watching and pointing and wondering, too.'

'You can see people wonder?' Jim said.

Freeman Grainger said, 'You can see it in their expressions every day in church.' Then he said, 'Why are you wearing a gun now, Jim?'

'It's Sam McRae's gun.'

'But you've never worn a gun.'

'I used to wear one all the time.'

'You did?'

'Uh-huh.'

'Well, why are you wearing one now in Parker's Crossing, I mean?' Grainger said.

'There's trouble coming,' Jim said.

'Exactly what folk are talking about,' Amos said. 'And by the way, Rose, this steak is delicious.'

'Thanks, Jim,' she said.

'Anyone asked you for money since I was away?' Jim asked.

'No,' she said.

The way she said it there were some unspoken words hanging in the air. Amos said, 'But Connery ran into a little trouble last night.'

Jim paused, his fork halfway to his mouth.

'Domino is a little smashed up, I hear,' Amos said.

'What happened?'

'Just a fight.'

'Nothing unusual there.' Jim ate the lump of steak off the end of his fork. It was indeed delicious. It was the finest steak. He'd asked for the best pieces, told Billy behind the counter that money was no object. Billy would tell Albert and between the two of them, all their customers would hear that money was no object for Junk Jackson. Sooner or later someone else — beyond Blue Garner and Henry Slade — would get interested. That was one way into the heads of whoever was chasing quick money in Parker's Crossing.

'No, but it was particularly wild, by all accounts,' Amos said. 'The place really got bust up and afterwards, so they tell me, no-one could quite figure out why it happened. Seemed like a couple of fellows got to fighting and pretty soon everyone was involved.'

'And the fellows that started it?'

'No-one seems to know. They did say a couple of the fellows from the Bridge Hotel were in there, though.'

'What makes you think it's linked to someone threatening Rose?'

'Nobody has actually threatened me.'

'You know what I mean.'

'This morning one of those fellows from the Bridge Hotel — fellow's got a hell of a scar — apparently said to Connery that he (Scarface) had struck a deal with the Sandersons down at The

Bridge to make sure that nothing like that happened there. Said if Connery wanted a little protection against *his* business going bust then maybe they could come up with a deal. Connery told him that it wasn't his business. The fellow said, well, a couple of nights like *that* and there wouldn't be a business and that would mean that Connery was out of a job.'

'I can imagine how Connery reacted to that.'

'They tell me that Connery took out his pick handle last night and laid into a couple of the Bridge fellows but one of them wrestled it away from him and used it on Connery. His head's a bit sore today and he wasn't in the best of moods. He threw Scarface out into the street by all accounts.'

Freeman Grainger said, 'Why is it always violence that people turn to?'

Jim looked at the young white-haired and pale-skinned man. He did genuinely look puzzled at the actions of his fellow man.

'They approached Father Thornley yet?'

'Who?'

'Whoever.'

'I don't think so.'

'And what would you and he do if they did?'

Amos said, 'If they asked you for money on account of if you didn't pay it, a bolt of lightning might just hit the church and burn it to the ground.'

'What are the odds of that?' Grainger said.

'Odds? Are you a gambling man?' Jim said.

'No. I mean, how likely is lightning?'

'With these fellows almost a certainty.'

'They wouldn't,' Rose said. 'Not the church.'

'I'm just asking the young fellow what he'd do if they did.'

'Well, we'd . . . talk to them. Try and show them the error of their ways.'

'And where would Thornley sleep after they'd burned the church down?'

'They'd do that?'

'Uh-huh.'

'So what can we do?' Grainger said.

'That,' Jim Jackson said, 'is why I'm now wearing a gun.'

9

Rivers ran a finger the whole length of his scar and said, 'There's money to be had here.'

Starling said, 'I think we've squeezed them pretty good. I could cut a few more throats and we might get some more, but there's no-one really rich here. You know, there ain't even a bank and the stagecoach is hardly worth bothering with.'

Rivers said, 'You're wrong.'

'About the stagecoach?'

'No. About there being nobody really rich here.'

Luke Hamilton said, 'The drunk fellow. The gunslinger.'

Rivers nodded. 'Uh-huh. Jackson. Shaky, they call him. Trembles, too.'

They were in the Bridge Hotel. It was early afternoon. Just the three of them. The other fellows — Burns and Laidlaw

— the two fellows that Ellie Sanderson had recommended would help them out with anything (in her words, *a little unto-ward*) hadn't been invited to the pow-wow.

Rivers was drinking water. Luke Hamilton had a coffee. Starling was downing whiskey.

'I didn't think he was that quick,' Starling said.

Rivers looked at him. 'Who said he was?'

'Lou said — '

'I said he was a gunslinger. Not a fast one,' Luke Hamilton said.

'He wasn't fast.'

'All of which is beside the point. He has money. Lots of money,' Rivers said.

'How do you know?' Starling asked. 'He don't look rich.'

'I talk to people,' Rivers said. 'He doesn't work. He drinks every day. He's been buying an awful lot of stuff. You heard what that fellow he shot said.'

'The one he trapped in the mine,' Hamilton said.

'Uh-huh. Word is that he keeps his

money in the mine. Lots of money.'

'You want me to bring him in?' Starling said. 'I can make him tell us where the money is.'

'No, you can't.'

'You saying I can't make him talk?'

'I'm not saying anything. The man is a trapper.'

'A trapper?'

'He set those fellows up. From what I can gather, he set them up good. You might be able to cut the truth out of him one finger at a time, but what you going to do if he's set up a ton of rocks right above *your* head when you lift up that bag of money?'

'It sounds like you've been thinking this one through,' Luke Hamilton said. 'Do you have a plan?'

'I do.'

★   ★   ★

Henry Slade wanted two things: more whiskey and some money to buy it with. In his sober moments he wanted

Blue back, too. So that was three things. But sober moments had been rare these last few days since he had watched Junk Jackson gun his friend down. Junk Jackson! Trembles. It hadn't meant to be this way. He and Blue should have been living the high life by now, living it up on Junk's money. How could it all have gone so wrong? How could such a shambolic wreck of a man turn the table on them out there at the mine and, as if that wasn't unreal enough, how did that drunkard turn into a deadly gunslinger in a matter of hours? It was wrong and it was impossible and most of all it was unfair. And on top of all that it seemed that Junk was suddenly a hero over at the Domino. Henry had been forced to take his drinking over to the Bridge Hotel where he didn't really have any friends — not that he'd had any other than Blue, which was why he wanted Blue back — and where the prices were higher and the shots smaller.

He kept seeing black, too. Seeing darkness. That was partly why he was drinking so much, trying to stay one step ahead of the blackness. It had caught up with Blue even before they had escaped the mine. Henry was damn sure it wasn't going to get him.

But now he'd run out of money. He'd run out of money the same day that Junk had rode back into town, no doubt having filled his pockets from his bottomless stash, and proceeded to buy clothes and food and get a haircut and a shave and even a knife. It was like the man was showing off.

Henry stood at the bar looking at his empty glass, his hands moving from pocket to pocket in the vain hope that he might find a coin.

'Another drink?' Wolfgang asked. It was early evening, there were few people in the Bridge bar yet.

'I'm . . . No, thank you,' Henry said.

'No money?'

'No money.'

'Mr Rivers would like to buy you one.'

'Mr Rivers?'

Wolfgang pointed with his chin to the smartly dressed man sitting over in the corner of the saloon. Henry had seen the fellow before. He had a scar. Some evenings he was in the lounge bar, some evenings in here with the rough guys. Usually he had a few fellows around him, but this evening he was on his own.

Seeing Henry looking over, Mr Rivers smiled and beckoned with his hand. Wolfgang placed a bottle of whiskey and a glass on the bar and said, 'Here, Mr Rivers is paying.'

Henry took the drink, walked across the room, placed the whiskey and glass on the table and sat down. Up close Mr Rivers looked a little older than he'd originally thought. There was grey in his thin beard and there were lines on his face, and that long scar looked old enough that Rivers could have been born with it. The man's eyes were grey, too, and though they twinkled a little in the late sunlight coming in low through the windows, there was a tiredness to them.

'Sit down, please,' Rivers said, smiling. But there was a tension in the smile — maybe brought on by that scar — and Henry found himself starting to rise again, suddenly worried that he shouldn't have sat before the man had made his invitation.

'I'm sorry. I — '

'I'm joking. I'm joking. Sit.'

Henry eased himself back down into his chair. Rivers reached across and popped the cork from the bottle, filled Henry's glass, and then topped up his own.

He put down the bottle and held out his hand.

'Rivers,' he said. 'Good to meet you.'

'Uh . . . Henry Slade.'

'You know who I am, Henry?'

'I've seen you in here.'

'I'm a business man. An investor.'

'OK.'

'In fact, in a way I'm like one of those forty-niners, used to be out there searching for the gold nuggets.'

Henry took a drink of whiskey. He

wasn't sure what the fellow was getting at.

'I think you might be able to help me find a particularly big nugget,' Rivers said.

'Me?'

'Yes.'

'I've never done any prospecting.'

'But you have. Maybe not for gold.'

'I don't understand.'

'Tell me about your friend.'

'My friend?'

'The one in the gunfight a couple of days ago.'

Henry took a deep breath. He didn't like to think about that gunfight. He drank some more whiskey and when he put his glass back on the table Rivers immediately filled it.

'Blue was a good guy. He was scared of the dark. He was . . . he was really mad and that's why he called Junk out. Junk trapped us back there in the mine and we had to dig ourselves out and it was pitch black and we didn't know if we were even going to make it. It drove

Blue a little wild. He was drunk and he was crazy and I don't think he was in any fit state to shoot it out like he did. I mean, any other time he'd have shot Junk dead easy.'

'What were you doing in the mine? Tell me about this Junk.'

'I don't know where he came from. But he turned up a while back and he ain't never done a day's work. He just drinks, yeah? It's like . . . He's always shaking. We call him Shaky. It's like he just wants to be drunk all the time. So we figured . . . You're not the law, are you, Mr Rivers?'

Rivers smiled and shook his head. 'No, I'm not the law, Henry. Far from it. Go on.'

'OK. So we — Blue and me — we figured Junk must have had a stash somewhere. You know, some money hidden away. And plenty of it. So we watched him. And sure enough, every so often he'd head off somewhere on that grey of his and then he'd take to drinking again for a few weeks.'

Rivers nodded and took the tiniest of sips from his whiskey. Outside Henry could hear horses and people and there was a breeze blowing into the saloon from the door and he could smell horse dung and something burning, or maybe cooking, and over at the bar Wolfgang was laughing with that little fellow Mingus. But it all felt remote and unreal. Talking about Junk Jackson, and what happened in that mine, and all about Junk's money was like going back in time a couple of days when he and Blue had it all figured out.

'So you followed him,' Rivers said.

'Yeah. He's got his money hidden out at . . . Hold on.'

'What is it, Mr Slade?'

'I'm telling you all this.'

'Yes, you are.'

'I mean, what's it worth?'

'Worth?'

'What I'm telling you. You can go and get that money. But by rights it belongs to me and Blue.'

'By rights?'

'Yeah.'

'So you want something for this information?'

'Yeah.'

'How about whiskey? Is my whiskey not enough?' The way he spoke, the way his eyes held Henry's eyes, Henry suddenly figured he may have over-stepped a mark he hadn't even seen. Especially as he'd already drunk plenty of the man's whiskey.

'Look . . . I mean . . . I'm not being funny. I . . . Blue's dead. It just seems if you get all that money and we — I — don't . . . It's not entirely right.'

'OK. I understand. It's a deal.'

'It's a deal?'

'Yes, it's a deal. You tell me what you know and I'll pay you.'

'You will?'

'Yes. Go on.'

'How much?'

'Carry on with your story, Mr Slade.'

There was that look again. Henry swallowed. 'He's got his money hidden over at Santiago. You know it?'

'I've heard of it.'

'The old copper mining town, half a day's ride north. There's nothing there now, just the old buildings. But that's where he went. He went into the mine itself.'

Henry paused. He didn't really want to think too much about the mine. He drank more whiskey. What with the darkness and with the way Rivers was looking at him, he needed it.

'Go on.'

'So we followed him inside. We found some money. He'd dropped a silver dollar. We knew we were close.'

More whiskey. He wondered if Rivers was as good as his word. Or was he giving away all he knew for nothing?

'And then?'

'Then he seemed to disappear and the roof collapsed and we were trapped.'

'He set you up.' Rivers was nodding as if Henry's words were agreeing with him.

'Yep. He set us up. He laid a trap.

And that's why Blue was so mad and that's why Blue died.'

'And how much money do you think this Junk Jackson has?'

'He's got enough for all of us, I reckon. Thousands, maybe. You seen him? He's been out at the mine and he's come back, and he's buying clothes and steaks and he's supposedly bought a ticket on the stage.'

'You think he's leaving?'

'I don't know. That's what folks say.'

'Is he married?'

'Married? No. He just turned up one day.'

'That's a shame. Does he have any close friends?'

'Only the saloon keepers. They like him. Oh, and that blind fellow that the Apache took care of. They're pretty close, I hear. He's probably a close friend. Yeah, him and that fellow are tight.'

Rivers nodded. 'He's pretty good with a gun, from what I saw.'

'Like I said, Blue was crazy. Crazy

and drunk. Any other time I don't think Junk would have stood a cat in hell's chance.'

'That aside, this Junk fellow was fast. I saw it.'

'Maybe.'

Rivers nodded. 'Anything else you know about him?'

'Not really.' He took a long, strengthening gulp of whiskey. 'Was it useful? I mean, what I've said.'

'Very.'

'Really?'

'Oh yes.'

'So you'll pay me? We've got a deal?'

'A hundred dollars. How does that sound?'

They, he and Blue, had thought they were going to get thousands.

'I was hoping — '

'And you can kill him,' Rivers said. 'A hundred dollars and you get to kill him.'

Now that Henry thought about it, that was a fourth thing. He wanted to kill Junk Jackson more than anything else. He'd have liked more than a hundred dollars, but he wasn't going to argue the point right now. Once he'd killed Jackson who knew how things might go down?

'Deal?' Rivers said.

'Deal.'

10

Amos was trying to figure out what day it was. It didn't matter as such, but a fellow liked to have something to hold on to. There was talk of getting a bell put in the church but so far nobody had figured out who should pay. At least with a bell folks would know when it was Sunday. That meal last night, that good steak that Jim had bought, that had felt like a Sunday meal. Sometimes, if he got up early enough and he was taking a coffee out on the boardwalk Amos could figure out a Sunday by it being slightly quieter than other days. Today he wasn't sure. It felt more like a week day.

He'd burned his hand on the stove and he was pretty sure there'd been something alive in the cup he'd picked up — maybe a spider or a lizard. But he'd tapped it out and made a coffee anyway. There wasn't anything a lizard could do to him that was a thousandth as bad as what had already been done to him. He knew he could have waited for Rose or Jim or Freeman, but a man needed some independence, and these early morning coffees were a rare pleasure, right up there with Jim reading *Moll Flanders* to him.

It was quiet, though. Maybe it was Sunday after all, he thought.

He put the coffee cup down on the little table that Rose had outside her door, pulled a handkerchief from his pocket and blew his nose, and he made his way back through the house and into Rose's yard, his hands stretched out before him and his feet shuffling along, feeling for obstructions. Everyone at Rose's was good — there was never anything out of place, there was never anything on the floor, and there was never anything not where it was supposed to be. If only the whole of the Crossing was like that he could have wandered round like a sighted man.

He made his way to the end of the yard, feeling and hearing Rose's hens flapping around his feet but not worrying about tripping over them. It was up to them to get clear of his feet. He opened the outhouse door and went inside. First thing he always did, every morning, was feel for the paper. Yes, there was some there. You didn't want to get caught out too often with no paper. He didn't know what paper it was — but the fact that it was there was good enough.

Little Joe Grubber — who one day would be a millionaire, of that Amos had no doubt — had taken to collecting all the waste paper he could find — newspapers and packaging and bill of sales and probably old wanted posters from Wagner's office — and he cut them up into squares then sold them round town as Little Joe's Outhouse Wipes. That, alongside his water business, meant Little Joe was probably making more money than many of the adults in the Crossing.

Amos undid the buttons on his breeches and sat down on the wooden bench, easing himself to just the right position over the hole. He breathed shallowly and through his mouth. Outside he heard one of Rose's hens squawk loudly.

Then he heard the scraping of wood on wood as the outhouse door was opened and he was rising up, trying to control the muscles in his belly that he had just been about to relax, and reaching down for his breeches. There was a rush of cool fresh air on his face and someone said, 'You make any sound at all and we'll cut your tongue out.'

'Who is — '

Someone punched him in the stomach and the air burst from his lungs. He staggered forwards, retching. He lost his footing and he tripped, his head cracked against the wooden door frame and in the darkness of his vision, he saw flashes of light and just for a moment those flashes were worth the pain. Then he was being pulled forward, tripping again, this time on his half-mast trousers and he could feel the chickens flapping by his feet and even in his disorientation and pain, he was sure there was more than one pair of hands yanking him out of the gate. A moment later he was lifted and dumped like a sack of feed across the saddle of a horse and somebody said, 'Go!' and then he was lurching forward, his breeches still halfway down his legs, and a rider alongside him gripping his shirt collar so he didn't slip off the horse.

For what seemed like a minute or two he thundered along, bouncing wildly, and then suddenly his horse stopped and he slid off, and his shoulder and his head and his hip all hit the ground hard.

'What the hell's going on?' His hip hurt, his shoulder hurt, his head hurt although those beguiling stars had vanished. And his stomach still hurt from the punch.

'Pull your trousers up, old man.'

He was already doing so.

They weren't in town anymore. As he did up his buttons he was listening and he couldn't hear anything. The breeze tasted fresher, too — although it always tasted good in the morning. But it had only been a few minutes at most. If he had had to bet some of Jim's money on it, he'd have said they were back in the trees where Jim had practiced his shooting just a few days ago.

'Now back on the horse, feller. This time you can sit.'

'Who are you?'

'Don't matter.'

Then someone was helping him up. Suddenly he felt a hand unwrapping the bandage from around his eyes.

'Hey, what you doing?'

'Shut up, old man.'

They took the bandage away and he felt a coldness where the bandage moisture evaporated from his skin. He always wanted to blink when he didn't have the damp bandage on.

Then they were away again, riding at

a moderate speed this time. Amos didn't know if any of them saw, and he didn't know if it would make the slightest bit of difference, but as they rode he pulled his handkerchief from his pocket and let it fall. It was actually a square of material from one of Rose's old dresses. She had torn the dress one too many times and had made some handkerchiefs and some dust-cloths from it instead.

'I still need my morning ablutions,' Amos said.

'Hold it in, feller,' someone said. 'We ain't stopping.'

And he felt the pace quicken.

⋆ ⋆ ⋆

Rose said, 'Amos is gone.'

She was standing in Jim's bedroom doorway.

'His coffee is outside half finished.'

'He'll be in the outhouse,' Jim said, rubbing his eyes. At least his head didn't hurt. One thing about not drinking was that your head didn't hurt in the mornings. 'He drinks half a cup and goes straight to his — '

'He's not there,' Rose said. The look in her eyes made Jim sit up and swing his legs out of bed. 'The door was open. The gate, too.'

Jim got to his feet, pulled his Levis over his under-trousers. Yesterday, no, the day before, he'd been up there at Santiago trying to figure out all the different ways things might go down, working to set up the time and place, trying to figure the future.

'How long has he been gone?'

'I heard him getting up an hour or so ago. He likes to be the first up, he likes the — '

' — smell of the fresh air in the mornings,' Jim finished.

'You think . . . He can't have gone far?'

'He's not *gone* anywhere. He's been taken.'

Son of a bitch. He'd been caught off-guard. He thought he had it all planned, sitting there talking to Wagner, working it out. Time and place. He'd drawn them out perfectly, that was the plan. It was just that they'd added in a variable — Amos — that he hadn't planned for. He should have thought of that. Them snatching Amos — it could just as easily have been Rose — before breaking cover. Wasn't that in all those engineering texts? Consider all your variables? Damn it.

Rose said, 'Who would want — '

'It's me. They want me and they know that Amos is my friend.' He looked at her. 'Thank goodness it wasn't you. Amos is tougher than they know.'

She said, 'You think I'm not tough?'

'I *know* you're tough. I wasn't meaning anything by it.'

Jim had his boots on now, and his over-shirt. He belted on McRae's gun. It felt good every time he wore that gun. But he felt angry with himself, too. He'd been over-confident and now? Now there was Amos to think of.

She said, 'You know I've got a gun?'

'You have?'

'Don't sound so surprised. It's only a parlour gun, but up close it's as good as anything. I'm a good shot, too. Was the best rabbit-killer in the wagon train when we rolled west all those years ago. And,' she said, 'I want you to promise me something.'

'Go on.'

'If someone has taken Amos and you find out who it is, you tell me. You promise now.'

He looked at her. 'That's not something I can promise. Killing isn't easy, Rose. People aren't rabbits. I wouldn't wish it on anyone. But what I will promise you is that they will pay. Whoever they are.'

★   ★   ★

They approached Jim within the hour. He was waiting for them, leaning impatiently on the railing outside Rose's, the place where he and Amos had spent most mornings drinking coffee and

172

talking. He cursed himself for not being there this morning when Amos had risen. But then Amos lived in a permanent darkness, sunrise meant little to him. He was an early riser who never saw the sun.

Jim saw them coming in the distance. Two of them. One was smartly dressed. The fellow with the scar who had been holding court in the Bridge Hotel the evening he and McRae had been in there. The other was one of the supposed-gun-slingers who had been standing around that evening.

They walked up to Jim and Scarface held out his hand and let a long narrow length of bandage unfurl.

'You shouldn't have taken that off him,' Jim said. 'He needs it to keep his eyes moist.'

The man ignored him. 'You and Starling here.' The man indicated the gunslinger who nodded at Jim. 'You two are going to take a ride.' Jim wondered if the nod was some kind of recognition following his exploits against Blue a few days back. One gunslinger to another. Or maybe it was just his imagination.

'Where's Amos?' Jim said, lighting up a cigarette.

'You can take your gun off and give it to me,' Scarface said.

Jim shook his head. He blew smoke into the space between him and the two men.

'You want to see Amos again?' the man said.

'You've got it wrong if you think Amos is some kind of lever over me.'

'Really?'

'Really.'

Scarface held up Amos's bandage again. He dropped it into the dirt. 'If he dies, it won't be easy.'

'What are you going to do? Cut his eyelids off and stake him out in the sun?' Jim saw the gunman, Starling, smile, albeit very briefly.

'You know we asked your landlady if she'd like a little protection.' It wasn't a question.

'She told me.'

'She said no. It would be terrible if something bad was to happen to her as well as Amos.'

'You think you've got all the aces?'

'We do, I'm afraid.'

Jim drew on his cigarette and looked at the man, seeing lines around his eyes that weren't made by the sun but by tension and worry. There was a tiredness in his eyes. But a hardness, too. He looked weary enough of life not to give a damn.

'I'm not giving you my gun. There are still Indians out there.'

'Starling will look after you.'

'I don't need looking after.'

'You give us what we want and we'll give your friend Amos back to you intact. Or as intact as he is.'

'I told you, Amos is nothing to me.'

'Yes, you did, and you were lying. Now, your gun, please.'

Jim blew more smoke between them. He dropped his cigarette onto the plank walk and ground it into dust with his heel. He looked at the dead cigarette for a few seconds to make sure he really had killed it. He'd heard of whole towns being burned down because fellows had dropped cigarettes on plank walks.

'Imagine Amos with his tongue cut out,' the man said. 'He can't see. Imagine him not being able to talk, either.'

'Imagine me hanging you by your thumbs from the nearest tree,' Jim said, and again he saw the briefest of smiles cross Starling's face.

'From what I hear you never had a gun until two days ago,' Scarface said. 'So I struggle to understand why you're so attached to it. Now, you give me the gun and then meet Starling up at the livery in ten minutes. Sooner we do this the better. You know it as well as we do.'

'I'll leave my gun here,' Jim said. 'I'm not giving it up to you.'

The man shrugged. 'Starling will search you. Any funny business and the only reason we'll keep you alive is so you can see your friend die first.'

'Ten minutes,' Jim said. He looked at

Starling. 'I'll see you there.'

The scarred man nodded. He and the one called Starling turned and left. Jim watched them for a few seconds then he stepped out into the road and picked up Amos's bandage.

* * *

Rose followed Jim to his room where he dropped Sam McRae's gun and belt on his bed. He was talking all the time he walked.

'They've got Amos,' he said. 'It's the same folk that threatened — or rather, *talked* — to you. They want me to go with them . . . Santiago, I guess.'

'Your money,' she said.

'Yep. And they release Amos.'

'Except they won't, will they?'

'I doubt it. They'll kill me. They'll kill Amos and then they'll carry on as they have been.'

Rose looked shocked and scared.

'Don't worry. It's not going to happen.'

She was looking at the gun on his bed. He took the knife he'd bought from Mulligan's and slid it down inside his boot. He was thinking again of the dime westerns. A knife wasn't a gun — and he was no knife fighter — but a knife surprise was better than no surprise. There would be other surprises, too.

'That's it,' she said. 'A knife?'

'Don't worry. Listen, go and tell Wagner what's happening. Tell him the plan is working and they've broke cover. Tell him I'm going to Santiago and I could use his help. Tell him to meet me at the mine — but tell him they've got Amos, too. We need to know where Amos is. They can't have taken him far. I think the fellow who's taking me wherever we're going mightn't be so bad. I might be able to find out where Amos is. When I come back we'll go and get him.'

'When you come back?'

'Rose . . . I'm no . . . I'm not . . . Look, they've upped the ante. If this Starling fellow tells me where Amos is, I will kill him and turn around and go and get Amos. What happens then will be up to them.'

'And if he doesn't tell you where Amos is?'

'Then . . . Then we play it out as we planned. Wagner and I will do what we need to do to bring these men to justice.'

'And Amos?'

'I don't know. Listen, maybe Julio is back. If he is he may be able to find Amos.'

'It sounds . . . It *doesn't* sound like much of a plan.'

'I know. Amos would agree.'

'In fact, it's no plan at all.'

'It's all we've got.'

He turned to her and smiled. She still looked scared and worried. He put his hands on her shoulders and said, 'It'll be all right. Listen, I can deal with any number of fellows at Santiago. Things are different now.'

'What do you mean?'

What he meant was that he'd killed a man, and once a fellow had stepped over that particular line, then he became a different person. He became the type that other men oughtn't to mess with.

'I'm different now,' was all he said.

★　★　★

'When we've got your money,' Henry Slade said, 'I'm going to personally take you down that damn mine and bury you alive, yeah? You see that I don't.'

The livery stable smelt of morning fresh feed. It wouldn't take long for the sweet scents to be overpowered by other smells. But for now it was reasonably pleasant, save for the fact that Henry Slade was sitting on a horse alongside the gunman called Starling. Jim Jackson couldn't figure out why they — Scarface and his crew — would have employed Henry Slade. Maybe Starling didn't know the way to Santiago?

'Thanks for the warning,' Jim said.

'Ain't a warning. It's a promise. I might even sit outside wherever I've buried you and listen to you beg.'

Mannie had already saddled up Jim's grey. When he brought the horse out he looked from Jim to Starling and then over at Slade.

'Things all right, Jim?' he said.

'Yeah, everything's fine,' Jim said.

'Best say your goodbyes to Shaky, Mannie,' Henry said. 'If that's what he means by fine.'

Jim looked at Mannie and shook his head as if to say *don't worry*. The simple movement riled Henry up a little more.

'I'm telling you, it's a promise,' he said. 'I'm going to do it for Blue.'

'That was a fair fight from what I saw,' Mannie said.

'Blue was still shook up from being trapped in the dark. Wasn't fair at all.'

Jim winked at Mannie.

'See you later, friend,' Jim said. Then he turned to Starling and asked, 'Where are we headed?'

Starling said, 'You tell me.'

Henry Slade said, 'Santiago.'

Jim said, 'Then Santiago it is.'

★   ★   ★

Rose was just back from Sheriff Wagner's office when Joe Grubber walked towards her back yard holding a chicken by the legs. The sheriff had said, 'The darn plan worked then,' when she told him they were forcing Jim to head over to Santiago.

'Yeah, but they've taken Amos,' she explained. Wagner admitted that complicated things a bit but he said he had faith in what Jim had done over in Santiago. 'What's he done over there?' she asked.

'Just prepared a few things.' Then he'd stood up, took his hat from a hook by the door, and said, 'I best get over there with him.'

That was a few minutes ago. Now her chicken squawked and twisted around and flapped its wings but Little Joe held on tight. He opened the gate, and came into the garden. Once the gate was closed he let go of the chicken and it flew from his hand and landed in the dust.

Joe counted the chickens in the yard.

'Six,' he said. 'One more to go.'

'I do appreciate it,' Rose said.

She hadn't asked Little Joe to round up her chickens — in fact, she had assumed that the birds were gone for good. But he had appeared a few minutes earlier with a chicken in each hand, his yellow hat low over his eyes as he was unable to push it back up on account of the chickens, and told her that he recognized them as hers. When she said she'd lost all of them he said he'd seen others working their way over towards the copse. He said he'd go and get them. It was on his third trip back that he asked how they'd got out and by the way where was Amos?

'Amos is always here drinking coffee and listening to the world,' Little Joe said. So she told him what had happened. 'This town is not good at the moment,' he said. Then he added, 'In fact, it's all wrong. But at least I can get your chickens for you.'

She watched him run back over to the trees. As far as she remembered his parents had a house — well, a shack — over on the south side of town where there was a lot of nothing. Some rough houses, some shacks, some tents. She recalled that his father occasionally drove a stagecoach and that his mother was a good seamstress. But maybe she recalled wrong. Perhaps it had been Little Joe's mother who had died from tuberculosis the winter before last? And perhaps his father wasn't the stagecoach driver. Maybe that had been someone else? Either way, Little Joe seemed to exist in a world of his own making. And in his own way he kept several elements of the town ticking over.

She wandered back inside the house and went upstairs to Jim's room. His gun was still on his bed. The town certainly was not good at the moment. Yet somehow that decline in the town's fortunes had changed Jim for the better. Good coming from evil, maybe. She'd always sensed there was more to him than he let on — although Amos told her most of what Jim told him, so she was aware of what he'd been through. It was a shame that people had had to die to help him change. But that wasn't his doing. It was as if he was changing to avenge them. There had been 'wrong' times before and they always passed, but this felt as if it was coming from within, not from outside when there was disease or Indians to cope with.

She slipped the revolver from its holster. It was heavier than she'd expected. A lot heavier than her own little pocket gun. It made what Jim had done out there on Main Street a few days before so much more impressive. She thought of him right now — being forced to take these men to wherever he had hidden his money. He hadn't seem bothered. In fact, quite the opposite; he had seemed calm and in control. But maybe he was putting on a face for her.

She put the gun back on the bed. Her husband came to mind. He was dead. She knew that. She'd always known that. Somewhere out there he had fallen, or starved, or got injured and caught a fever. There were a dozen, a score of ways it could have happened. She would never know how, but she *knew*. And yet here she still was in Parker's Crossing. She could go out to the coast and live with her children anytime she wanted, yet she was still here. Why? She wasn't sure that she knew the answer. Maybe it was because this was the last place she knew with her husband. Or maybe it was because there was always an Amos, or a Jim, or a Little Joe —

'Missy Rose! Missy Rose!'

It was Little Joe Grubber now, calling her from downstairs.

She went downstairs and he was in the kitchen doorway and he had a square of cloth in his hand, a blue and white square.

'This was in the trees,' he said.

'It belonged to Amos,' she said, and her heart started to pound a little harder than the rush down the stairs warranted. 'I made him handkerchiefs from an old dress.'

Little Joe looked at her.

'They took him into the trees,' she said.

'And he left us this,' Joe added. Then he said, 'Let me go get Ghost.'

★   ★   ★

Starling said, 'That was pretty good shooting the other day.'

They were riding side by side. Working their way towards the distant pinewoods. Henry Slade was behind them. Every few minutes Jim heard Henry mumble and moan and sometimes when the words were loud enough, he realized that Henry was still threatening him, still listing ways to kill Jim.

'Wasn't much competition.'

'You didn't know that, though,' Starling said. Jim glanced across at him. The man didn't look any more than about twenty-five. Clear eyes and no grey in the stubble on his chin. He was staring back at Jim, interested, friendly.

'I guess not.'

'I counted three shots.'

'Blue was still in shock,' Henry Slade said from behind them. 'It wasn't a fair fight.'

'Always best to make sure,' Jim said.

'You a gunman by trade?' Starling asked him. 'You know what I mean.'

'You shouldn't be talking to him,' Slade said. 'He's the enemy.'

They both ignored Slade. 'Train robber,' Jim said.

'Train robber? I'll be damned.'

'If you're caught you will be.'

'They caught you?'

'Uh-huh.'

'Hard-time?'

'Ten years. The hardest.'

'Rivers won't like you talking to him.

He ain't here as a friend,' Slade said.

'Rivers?' Jim said.

'The fellow who was with me earlier.'

'Scarface.'

'Yep.'

'How did he get that scar?'

'No idea. I think he's had it since he was a kid. He don't say. Luke says he heard that Rivers's own father did it to him.'

'What's his story?' Jim said.

'Story?'

'You fellows taking money off folks in town who can't afford it.'

Starling looked at him for a long time. The morning sun lit his face on one side, his hat cast a shadow over his forehead.

'You used to take money off the folks on those trains?' Starling said eventually.

'Yep.'

'Why?'

'Because he's a son of a bitch,' Slade said.

'I was building a stake.'

'Ain't we all?'

'Had a girl back East. Rich girl.'

189

Starling smiled. 'They're never worth it.'

'This one was.'

'Worth all that hard time?'

Jim thought about it. For many years he had thought about it and he didn't really need to think about it anymore. Yet he still did. Every day.

'If I thought I'd ever see her again then yes, it was worth it.'

'But I'm going to bury you alive,' Henry Slade said. 'So I guess that means it wasn't worth it.'

★   ★   ★

Ghost said, in his quiet boyish voice, 'See right there. The horses pushed away right there. Three, I'd say. Heading that way.'

Little Joe Grubber and Rose looked the way Ghost was pointing. Through the trees and beyond.

'We need horses,' Rose said. She had put on a pair of Levis and a blue shirt and boots. Around her waist she had

190

strapped Jim's — McRae's — gun. It felt incongruous. It felt heavy. When she had first caught up with them in the copse Little Joe had looked at the gun, had blown his breath out through pursed lips in a silent whistle, and said nothing.

He said, 'You coming with us?'

'Darn right.'

'And you have horses?'

'Nope.'

'Then we'll have to run,' Ghost said.

Rose wasn't exactly sure how old she was. She reckoned about forty, give or take five years. But some days she felt younger. Some older. One thing she knew, she wasn't going to be able to run through the morning heat and keep up with a couple of kids who spent all day every day running.

'You go ahead. I'll go and see Mannie. I'll catch you up.'

'We might be out of sight,' Little Joe said.

'There's a whole lot of nothing on the other side of these trees. I'll see you.

If you think you're going somewhere where I won't, then wait for me.'

'OK,' Little Joe said. 'But be quick. Amos left us a sign. He wants us to save him.'

★ ★ ★

Rivers looked at his pocket watch. It was an Elgin railroad watch he'd taken off a man Starling had shot dead on a bank robbery about a year before. The robbery hadn't netted them as much as they would have liked, but it had been enough. It had kept Mr Smith, back in Santa Fe, happy. Or as happy as he ever was. It wouldn't be long before all debts were settled and then he, Rivers, would be free to keep all of the money he unearthed. There'd be a place some-where, not like this hole, but somewhere big enough that he and Starling could make a very good living doing exactly what they were doing here. Here it was just a way of passing the time whilst looking out for the big money. Scare people. Hurt a couple, kill a few if need be, and watch the money roll in. But elsewhere, in the right place, with the right city, it could be a gold mine.

He clicked the pocket watch closed. It was time to go. Hamilton and those two boys Ellie had set them up with would be well away with that blind fellow by now, and Starling and Henry Slade would be heading off with Junk Jackson, riding over to Santiago.

Rivers absent-mindedly ran a finger down the length of the scar on his face. Actually, he wasn't sure if it would be a good thing to stick with Starling after this job. The kid enjoyed killing people just a little too much. It wasn't that he didn't trust Starling. The kid was a good one. He did what he was told and he was very quick with a gun. It was just he was starting to enjoy the violence too much. Take the other night, the night they had killed McRae.

They had known that somebody was tracking them. Mr Smith had tele-graphed them back in Paradise, the previous town along the trail. Mr Smith was like a spider in the centre of a web. Right there in Santa Fe but with a whole network of people criss-crossing the territory working for him, sending money back to him the way Rivers was. All probably massively in debt to him, too, just like Rivers. He didn't know how Smith had known about the bounty hunter, but the telegraph had said it was time to move on, that there was someone on their trail. Starling had been ready to kill the fellow there and then, but it hadn't been right.

They didn't know who the fellow was, for one thing. But here in Parker's Crossing it was different. Mr Smith knew the Sandersons — maybe, Rivers often thought, Smith even owned the Bridge Hotel — and they were able to set up a nice little base and do the job right. Several times over the last week they'd had Mingus, the little guy, tell any fellow that they suspected of being the unknown bounty hunter that Rivers and his boys were planning to move out in the middle of the night. A couple of times the fellow Mingus told was kind of puzzled and that was that.

But the other night, when he told the same thing to McRae, they hit pay dirt. Three in the morning, as Rivers pretended to sneak out of the back of the hotel there was McRae with a gun, saying, 'Hold up, Rivers, if you're going anywhere it's back to Texas with me.' So Rivers had put his hands up and when McRae had come closer — a pair of handcuffs in his hands — Starling stepped out of the shadows and hit McRae upside the head so hard he didn't even grunt before he hit the ground. And later, when they hauled him over to the bridge Rivers swore that Starling actually smiled as he cut McRae's throat. Starling looked so young and kind, too. He reminded Rivers of Mr Smith. Not the young and kind bit, but the fact he enjoyed killing so much. That was why you always repaid Mr Smith. If you didn't he'd kill you, or have you killed, and guaranteed it wouldn't be easy.

So maybe Starling was getting to be too much of a risk? But then, you needed someone like that. Someone who didn't care about killing and hurting people.

Hamilton was different. Luke Hamilton was as straight up as they came. Tough, sure. Fast, yep. But he was Smith's man. He was both a bodyguard to Rivers — making sure nothing happened to Rivers and that cash flow back to Santa Fe dried up — and a prison guard — ensuring Rivers didn't just try to disappear without repaying all those debts. As soon as this score was done, or maybe the next, and they had enough money, he and Starling and Hamilton would take it back to Santa Fe and that would be that. They'd never see Hamilton again. He'd be off watching some other debtor. And that time was getting close. Rivers could feel it in his bones.

Rivers stood up. It was time to go and get his horse and go and watch the fun.

11

Starling said, 'I knew a feller who swore that a cross draw was quicker. He was right handed but wore his gun on his left hand side facing backwards.'

'I've never really thought about it,' Jim Jackson said.

'We tried shooting bottles. I won. Though he says he won.'

'Bottles don't shoot back.'

'Exactly. But short of going up against each other, how would you tell?'

Jim Jackson looked across at Starling. They were riding through the trees up on the rise above the Santiago valley. The foliage cast shadows across the gunslinger's face and his hat was pulled low enough that Jim couldn't see his eyes clearly. But there was a shape to the man's posture, the roll of his shoulders. Jim had seen it before back in the prison camps when a couple of fellows were shaping up to fight each other and no-one — maybe not even the fellows in question — yet knew.

'I figure that a fellow whose gun is pointing backwards is going to have to spend precious time turning it around.'

'Exactly. Like I said, I reckon I won.'

'I'm sure you did.'

'There ain't many faster than me.'

'I'm sure you're right.'

Henry Slade had ridden on ahead. He had stopped where the tree line finished and was silhouetted against the blue sky. He turned now and said, 'Where you got the money hidden then, Shaky? Still in the mine?'

'Probably ain't many faster than you, either,' Starling said.

'I can out-shoot most bottles, that's for sure.'

'I'm probably faster than you,' Starling said. 'But I've got the advantage that I've seen you shoot and you haven't seen me. So I know that I'm faster and you just have to trust my judgement.'

'Can't argue with that,' Jim said.

'Plus,' Starling said, 'I actually like killing people. A lot of folks, they hesitate. See, they don't really want to kill someone.'

'You've seen a lot of gunfights?' Jim asked.

'Enough.'

'So you probably saw me hesitate then. I didn't really want to kill Blue.'

He looked back over at Starling and smiled.

'Once I give you the money perhaps we can go and shoot some bottles?' Jim said.

⋆　⋆　⋆

They brought their horses to a halt outside McCourey's saloon. Jim Jackson couldn't feel any breeze but the swing door still swung gently, squeaking with every moment.

'Here we are then,' he said.

'Where's the money?' Henry Slade said.

'Where's Amos?'

'Amos is back at a place just north of town,' Starling said. 'An old shack. A nice place to be honest. Three rooms and a porch. But deserted. I think the folks got scared off by the Apache.'

'Is it painted green?' Slade asked.

'Yeah.'

'That's the old Slater place,' Slade said. 'They weren't scared off by the Apache. They were killed by the Apache.' He looked over at Jim. 'So where's the money?'

'How do I know Amos is going to be OK?'

'What value is there in killing him?' Starling said.

'You told me you like killing people.'

'It's a good point. But I'll make an exception for a blind old man.'

'The money,' Slade said. 'Is it in the mine?'

'And me?' Jim said, looking at Starling.

'I like you.'

'But you're not sure, are you?'

200

'Of what?'

'Whether you're faster than me or not.'

'I'm sure.'

Jim smiled. 'No, you're not. And that's going to bother you every day.'

'Henry wants to know where the money is,' Starling said.

'It's right here,' Jim said. 'The first bag anyway.'

'What do you mean, the first bag?' Slade said.

'I'd be a fool to hide it all in one place, wouldn't I? What if somebody found it by accident?'

'How many bags are there?' Starling asked.

'Four.'

'How much money?'

'Five hundred in each. At least.' Jim Jackson had no idea if this was true. He'd never counted the money. But it wasn't a made-up figure. Back when they used to share out the spoils of their train robberies at the small adobe farmhouse in the Texas wilderness, the money was split in hundreds of dollars each. It mounted up very quickly. And it was one of the very small mercies of his recent life that when Sam McRae and his partners turned up to arrest Jim Jackson, Jim was planning that very day to go and recover the money that he kept hidden in a couple of saddlebags in a tiny west Texas cave. If they'd have caught him two hours later they'd have had the money, too.

'Two thousand dollars in all?' Henry said.

'At least,' Jim said. 'You want me to go and get the first one?'

'No,' Starling said. 'Henry can go. Where exactly is it?'

'Upstairs. First room on the right at the top of the stairs. There's an iron bedstead in there and an old wooden wardrobe. Open the wardrobe — it's empty. But the base is loose. Lift it up and you'll find the bag.'

'It better be there,' Henry said.

'If it isn't then someone's had a lucky find,' Jim said.

Henry swung off his horse.

'And don't get any funny ideas,' Starling said, looking at Henry.

Henry looked back at him, nodded, and then pushed his way through the saloon doors which squeaked more loudly for a moment.

'You don't seem bothered,' Starling said to him.

'About what?'

'About any of it. About us taking your money. About him thinking he's going to kill you.'

'*Thinking* about it?'

Starling shrugged. 'Maybe he'll do more than think about it. But my point remains — why aren't you bothered?'

'The day is young,' Jim said.

'Meaning I should be on my guard.'

'Things change,' Jim said.

'You know they'll kill Amos if you do anything stupid.'

'Like I said to you back in town, why do you think Amos is any hold over me?'

'The boss thinks so.'

'If I was you I'd take $500 and just ride on.'

'You said there were four bags.'

'I'm offering you one. Take it and go.'

'You're the one doing the bargaining now, huh?'

Jim smiled. He looked at the swinging doors of the dilapidated saloon through which Henry Slade had gone. He looked across at the mine buildings nestling up against the far valley wall. Now he could feel the breeze on his face. It was cool and refreshing.

He held out his hands.

'See these?'

'What about them?'

'Steady as a rock.'

'You know you talk in riddles?'

'Five hundred is a good deal. If I was you — '

From inside the saloon came a shriek and then they heard Henry Slade yell, 'You son of a bitch!' and then they heard a door slam and a few seconds later they heard him cry out again, this time followed by the sound of wood splintering and a huge crash.

'What have you done?' Starling said.

Jim Jackson looked back at him. There was a gun in Starling's hand. Jim had only looked away for a second. The man was quick.

'I did nothing,' Jim said. 'You have to be careful with these old buildings. Want me to go and take a look?'

'No.'

He could see the indecision in Starling's eyes. There was silence from inside the old saloon now.

'What we going to do?' Jim asked. 'Sit here all day?'

'Off your horse.'

As Jim climbed off his horse Starling did the same. Still holding the gun pointing towards Jim Jackson, Starling pulled a coil of rope from the back of his saddle.

'Hands out,' he said. He slipped his gun back into his holster and started tying Jim Jackson's hands.

★ ★ ★

Starling pushed open the door to the saloon. It squeaked, and when the squeak died he heard Henry Slade moaning quietly somewhere in the darkness ahead of him. The air was filled with dust and the light coming through the dirty windows looked like solid lines of white paint.

He drew his gun again and edged slowly, very slowly, into the building.

As his eyes adjusted to the contrast between the shadows and the light, Starling saw ahead of him tables and chairs, some overturned, while most were filthy with dust but one was clean and even had an empty bottle, a glass, and a plate on it, as if someone had enjoyed a meal there recently.

There was a wooden staircase leading up to the first floor but as he got closer, Starling saw that the top few steps were gone. Instead there was just a gaping hole.

He's a trapper.

You had to hand it to Mr Rivers, he was sharp. He saw things, and thought things through, far better than he,

Starling, could. Take that idea of just asking people if they'd like to pay to be looked after. It wasn't illegal. It was just them looking after people. And if a few bad things happened to people to make them consider taking up the offer then that was just . . . well, that was where he came in. But it was a brilliant idea. And here, sending this Henry Slade along to walk right into Jackson's trap had been a brilliant idea, too.

There was Henry Slade, lying on the floor, amongst the wreckage of the stairs, blood on his face. His legs twisted beneath him.

'Son of a bitch put rattlesnakes in the bag,' Henry said, when he saw that it was Starling who had come for him.

Starling moved some timber from across Henry's torso.

'Jesus! Easy,' Henry said.

'What happened?'

'The bag . . . the cupboard was right where he said. When I lifted up the wood at the base of the cupboard I heard something move — not snakes. I mean, he'd connected something to that wood. Then there was the bag. So I picked it up — '

'You opened it?'

'I wanted to make sure he wasn't tricking us.'

'And there was no money?'

'It was full of rocks and rattlesnakes. One of the sons of bitches bit me. You're going to have to help me get back to the doc. I think my leg's broke, too. Maybe both of 'em. Jesus, they hurt! When I came back out — I was running on account of that snake — the stairs gave way. It was all right going up.'

'He's a trapper,' Starling said.

'He's what?'

'Nothing.'

'Help me up.'

'Can you walk?'

'I can feel the poison in me. We need to get back. Hey . . . what are you doing? I'm on your side.'

Starling shot Henry Slade between the eyes and turned and headed back outside.

12

Jim's hands were tied tightly and the rope was then knotted to the pommel of his saddle. Jim Jackson pondered on walking the mare away from McCourey's saloon and then trying to work the knot loose. He still had the knife in his boot — Starling had been careless and not searched him, despite Rivers saying to do so — but the knife was, for the moment, useless. He'd tried but the way his hands were tied he couldn't get his fingers down inside his boots. But he knew it was pointless simply to walk away whilst still tied up. Starling had only been in the building less than a minute when he'd shot Henry Slade — at least that's what Jim Jackson assumed the shot was about. It was clear on the ride up here that Henry Slade was nothing more than an irritant to Starling. Jim had pondered on why the fellow was even here. Now he realized that they were ahead of him in that regard, too.

Starling came back outside.

'You're a clever son of a bitch, aren't you?'

He still had the gun in his hand. There were wisps of smoke coming from the barrel.

'You shot him?'

'He was dying anyway. It was a mercy killing.'

Jim looked at Starling, seeing the young man in a new light. Seeing the coldness in the man's eyes, the slight smile and the glow to the man's face in the aftermath of a killing. It occurred to Jim that he, too, could die out here today. It had all seemed so easy, smoke them out, set up the time and place, and watch them walk into the trap. Except they had been ahead of him and now it was he who was trapped. But he knew if he could play for time then Wagner would be here. The sheriff would pretty quickly cotton on to what was happening and between them they could play it out so Wagner got behind Starling and either shot him, or caught him.

That would be one down.

Starling walked over to his horse, took a skin from the back of the saddle and drank water. He didn't offer Jim any.

'Going to be a hot day,' he said.

'You want me to tell you where the money really is?' Jim Jackson said. He was resisting the urge to look left to glance way up on the hillside to the tree line. His peripheral vision told him there was movement up there. Wagner. He didn't want to give Starling cause to look that way.

'Can do if you like.'

'Isn't that why we're here?'

'It certainly is.'

'You don't seem in a hurry,' Jim said. The urge to look up at the slope was unbearable.

Starling drank more water. It ran from his mouth. It looked cool. Jim

Jackson could feel the heat of the midday sun on his shoulders.

'No, there's no hurry.'

No hurry was good. It would give Wagner time to get in position. But now there was a knot of fear growing in Jim's stomach. It felt like things were just getting away from him a little. That all his plans, all his carefully laid preparations might stand for nothing. Tied up he felt helpless, the way he'd felt every day for ten years back in the Texas system. Even just thinking such things made him shake and yearn for a drink. After they'd killed McRae, after *he'd* killed Blue Garner then he thought things had changed. These last few days he'd felt different. Brave. Invincible, even. He'd felt like a man again. But now . . . now he was just starting to wonder if it hadn't all been an illusion brought on by killing a man. Maybe he had been imagining himself to be something that he wasn't. That, after all, he was still Junk Jackson and the rest was all a dream.

He pushed the thoughts away. But he could feel his arms start to tremble.

'You going to untie me? You were happy to have me riding free all the way here.'

'Nope and yep.'

'Can I have some water?'

'Nope.'

'So what are we doing?'

What they were doing was standing by their horses outside the abandoned saloon in the blazing sun.

'Waiting.'

'For what?' Jim said. He could feel more uncertainty rising now. *He* was waiting for Wagner. Who was Starling waiting for?

'The boss — Mr Rivers — said you were a trapper.'

'A trapper?'

'That you'd set traps to protect your money.'

'Oh.'

'I told him that I could get you to tell us all about those traps.' As he talked Starling hung the water skin back on his saddle and now pulled a knife from a sheaf. 'I believe I could get you to tell me everything.'

Jim Jackson felt a physical memory in his belly, in his bowels. It was the memory of all those beatings when he had been a prisoner. The way they had broken him — broken him easily. He would have told everything he knew back then.

'But the boss said no. He thought — '

'He knew I would tell you nothing,' Jim said, using all his focus to make his words sound stronger than his body felt. He willed himself not to tremble. It was as if all the good stuff that had happened recently — all the stuff that had started when he had gunned down Blue Garner — was being washed away.

'No, he thought I might kill you and then we'd never know where the money was. So we wait.'

Now the movement on the far slope was more than just peripheral vision. Without turning his head Jim could see that it wasn't Wagner. It was three men, no, four.

When he could bear it no longer he turned to look.

It was three of the men from the Bridge, not the one with the scar — Rivers — but the others. And in the middle of their line of horses they had Amos.

* * *

The way Sheriff Wagner figured it you didn't want to do the obvious, didn't want to show your cards too early as it were. He'd been in enough situations in his life where walking straight out into situations might have been brave but it sure was foolish, too. And the older he grew the wiser he got. So when Rose told him that they — whoever *they* were, because they still didn't really know — had taken Amos and were forcing Jim to ride over to Santiago and dig up his money and give it to them, he was both pleased and perturbed. Pleased because it meant their plan was working. Perturbed because *they* had added an extra complexity, an extra level of careful thinking to it. In a way it was symptomatic of what they were doing around town — it was a cleverly thought out way to make money.

So he had to be clever, too. And that meant he better not do the obvious and ride as fast as he could to Santiago. Oh he needed to get there quickly, but you didn't survive a War — two wars if you included the Indian wars — and all these years wearing a badge by blundering in. No, he'd best take care.

He took his six-gun and two rifles and a knife, handcuffs and rope.

He took a trail that ran a little ways north of the direct route between Parker's Crossing and Santiago, and whenever his trail ventured out into the open or wound a little close to the main trail, he stopped and paused and watched. Sometime it felt like he was being a silly old fool, wasting time for no good reason.

But it was at one of these pauses, whilst he sat quietly by the trees rolling a cigarette, watching and listening, that he saw the four riders coming along the main trail.

'I'll be damned,' he said quietly to himself and even allowed a smile to cross his lips. If he'd have ridden the main trail then all those riders would have come up behind him at some point.

Initially he wondered if they were even anything to do with his and Jim's situation. They might just be chancers from the Crossing heading out to Santiago to try their luck and finding this fabled money. But then, as they came closer to where he sat quietly — cigarette unlit — in the shadows he saw that it was some of the fellows from the Bridge Hotel. Three of the young fellows. They all had guns on their hips.

In the midst of them all was Amos, his sightless eyes un-bandaged. He was moaning at them, telling them he needed to stop because his belly wasn't going to hold on much longer and Wagner wasn't sure but didn't Amos turn and look directly at him, or at the place where he was hidden?

Wagner touched his own six-gun.

But no, he might get one or two of them. But all three? The odds were against it. Better to maintain the element of surprise.

So he let them pass. A few minutes later he smoked his cigarette and only once he finished his smoke did he ride after them, keeping his distance.

★ ★ ★

'Don't do it,' Amos said. 'Don't give 'em a nickel.'

He was standing just a few feet from Jim Jackson. The two gunslingers from the Bridge Hotel were standing either side of Amos and the other one that had ridden in with him was talking to Starling.

'Where's Henry?' the new rider said.

'Dead,' Starling said, and nodded towards Jim who was still tied to his horse.

'The drunk killed him?'

'The boss was right. He set a trap.

Henry walked straight into it.'

Amos said, 'Don't worry about me, Jim.' One of the gunslingers holding him said shut up and the other spat a stream of tobacco juice onto the floor.

Now the one talking to Starling turned to Jim and said, 'How many more traps have you set?'

Jim said, 'Untie me.'

'Not a chance.'

'You're that scared of me?'

'We're not scared of you at all,' Starling said.

'Then untie me. What am I going to do? There's four of you.'

'How many traps?' the other said.

'There's four bags of money. I already told your pardner that. Traps by two of them.'

'I don't believe you.'

'We'll get the blind fellow to pick up the bags,' Starling said. 'See if what happens to Henry happens to him.'

'Where's the first bag?' the other said.

'Untie me. I have something for Amos.'

'What?'

'His bandage. You sons of bitches threw it in the dirt. How would you like to have no eyelids?'

Starling and the new rider looked at one another. The new rider nodded.

Once he was untied Jim rubbed his wrists and then reached in a pocket for the long bandage.

'I need water.'

'Why?'

'You threw it in the dirt for one thing. And the whole point of it is that it needs to be wet.'

Starling handed Jim the water skin he'd been drinking from. 'Don't waste it.'

Jim poured water onto the bandage and watched it splash onto the ground. He heard Starling curse him. The man had been quite friendly on the ride up to Santiago. Now, in front of his colleagues, his tone was harsh and mean.

Jim walked over towards Amos. The two fellows holding him let him go.

Amos's legs buckled a little but he steadied himself, reaching out a hand towards where Jim was coming towards him.

'You OK, Amos?'

'I ain't even had my morning rituals yet. Damn fellows took me right off the hole.'

Jim smiled and he wrapped the bandage around the old fellow's head.

Amos whispered, 'There's someone else coming. I heard 'em breathing when we passed by a mile or so back. Wagner, I think. I could smell his tonic, too.'

'It'll be all right,' Jim whispered as he secured the bandage. Then louder, 'How's that?'

Amos said, 'Almost as sweet as when Rose does it.'

The new rider next to Starling said, 'I heard you like to stand on the plank walk and drink coffee most mornings, old fellow.'

'You talking to me?' Amos said.

'Uh-huh.'

'The name's Amos.'

Now the man looked at Jim, 'So, Shaky — OK if I call you that? — where's the money? Four bags, you say? So let's keep it easy and quick. You tell us where the bags are, Amos can get them.'

'And if I don't care to keep it easy and quick?'

'Then we'll cut off Amos's thumbs. Starling here will enjoy that. No more holding coffee cups in the morning.' He paused. 'So . . . quick and easy?'

'Quick and easy,' Jim said.

⋆   ⋆   ⋆

'We're going to need a board,' Jim said.

'A board?' the other said.

'Amos is going to need to stand on something if he doesn't want to fall in the hole.'

Jim had led them all around the back of McCourey's saloon. He'd pointed out where a bag of money was hidden in the roof of the outhouse. To reach the money one would need to stand on the sitting board. Jim Jackson had cut through several of the supports holding that sitting board in place. Anyone standing on it would cause the board to give way and deposit them in the deep hole. At least it was dry, Jim thought. It didn't smell and it wasn't deep enough to kill or trap anyone. But had things played out differently it would have given Jim more than enough time to take advantage of the situation.

Jim had a board exactly the right size already hidden in a room within McCourey's. He'd figured that there might be a time when he'd need to recover that money quickly. So he found some appropriate timber and hid it away.

Now he said, 'Want me to go inside and find something?'

'No,' the other said. 'Burns, Laidlaw. The old man — Amos — isn't going anywhere. See what you boys can find inside.'

'Watch out for snakes,' Jim said. 'I'd hate to be blamed if you guys inadvertently step on a rattler.'

The two cowboys went inside McCourey's. Jim figured that it wouldn't take them too long to find some wood, but every second was a second more for Wagner to get here. What he needed to do was to get close enough to grab one of these fellows' guns from right out of his holster once the sheriff showed up. But looking up at the hill there was no sign of him yet. Timing was going to be everything.

Burns and Laidlaw came out a few minutes later carrying a door.

'We had to rip it off its hinges,' one of them said, the one who was chewing tobacco. Jim didn't know if it was Laidlaw or Burns. The same man said, 'Henry's in there, Luke. He's been shot.'

The one called Luke looked across at Starling.

Starling shrugged. 'He got bit by a rattler and fell through the floor and busted his leg. He was going to die anyway.'

Luke said, 'You're a cold-hearted son of a bitch, aren't you?'

Starling smiled.

Luke turned to Amos and said, 'Time for you to go into the outhouse, old man. You've been wanting to all morning.'

★   ★   ★

The one called Burns held Amos's legs as he balanced on the door they'd placed across the outhouse sitting board. Amos reached up and blindly felt around for the bag of money that Jim had said was up there. His whole body ached. He was old enough that a ride of a couple of hours would have caused him to ache anyway, but they'd punched him and he'd fallen off a horse and hit his head and shoulders and hip and the aches were just not giving in. They were getting worse. When he stretched for the money bag he could feel muscles and tendons that he hadn't used in years creaking and groaning and complaining.

He couldn't help but wonder if there was going to be a snake curled up there in the roof space. Or maybe a spider or two. He knew that Jim wouldn't have sent him up there if there was any further trap, but those critters had a way of finding their way into places you didn't want them to. He couldn't help but wonder about Jim. These fellows had the drop on him, but he didn't seem too bothered. There was a hint of resignation and weariness in his voice, but he'd said it'd be all right so he must have something more up his sleeve. Thing was, there were four of them, and even if it was Wagner back there in the trees — and there was no saying it was, it could have been a heavy breathing cougar for all Amos knew, although there weren't many cougars that wore Caribbean rum tonic as a way of hiding uncleanliness — what could one old sheriff do to help Jim out of this situation?

He stretched up and something pinged around his ribcage.

'Damn,' he said, and pulled a face.

'What is it?' Burns said.

'My ribs hurt.'

'You got the money?'

'Right here,' Amos said as his fingers around a bag. 'Figure you boys is going to be very rich very soon.'

★   ★   ★

Outside, when the one called Luke opened the bag, they all started to whoop and holler. A heavy feed sack inside another feed sack, and the inner one was full of silver dollars, eagles and half-eagles, some bank-notes, and some rings, and a pocket watch and even a couple of actual gold nuggets.

'Hot damn,' Laidlaw said and grinned at Burns.

'No wonder you never did a day's work in your life,' Luke said, looking at Jim.

'Three more bags,' Starling said and when he caught Jim's eyes, Jim knew that the man didn't believe him. Starling thought there might be more and Jim knew that if things got to that stage then Starling would most likely cut him — or Amos — in an effort to make sure there wasn't a fifth, or sixth, bag.

'Three more,' Jim said.

'Hot damn,' Laidlaw said again.

★   ★   ★

Sheriff Wagner sat quietly in the tree line looking down upon Santiago. It had been a while since he had been here but the place rarely changed. A bunch of buildings, all abandoned, some close enough to each other to form little clusters with roads and alleyways between them, most spread out thinly. And the main road leading up to the mine across the valley.

He watched the men in the distance outside one of the bigger buildings. His eyesight wasn't so good these days but damn it if that wasn't Amos Dunkley down there. What in the hell was going on? Rose had said they'd kidnapped Amos and were thus forcing Jim to ride with them to Santiago and to get his money. Last thing he had expected was to see so many people down there, and one of them being Amos. It put a different complexion on things. Rose had said that they wouldn't let Jim take his gun — well, that was obvious — but if he could get close enough and get his six-gun to Jim then . . . Well, if he could take out one or two with his rifle, Jim would do the rest. Hell, if he could get his six-gun to Jim then the fellow would probably take care of it on his own. How many were down there? There was Amos, and there was Jim, and that left . . . one, two, three, four of 'em. Four oughtn't to be a problem.

Jim had said to meet him at the mine. OK, so that's what he'd do. Maybe Jim was leading them there slowly, giving him — Wagner — time to get there. He'd have to take a wide loop around the town, but he could do it. Leave his horse somewhere and sneak up on foot. But he could do that, too.

Yeah, it would work.

Except . . . Except there was something niggling the back of Sheriff Wagner's mind and he couldn't quite work out what it was.

The answer came with the ratchet of a gun being cocked and someone saying, 'You move even an inch and you're dead.'

13

'Next bag,' the one called Luke said.

'Up along the street,' Jim said. 'Third building on the left. Looks like it was a bunkhouse or maybe a cathouse.'

'Where's the money?'

'In the outhouse.'

'Again?' Starling said.

'Saves me having to remember lots of different places.'

'You sawn through the boards this time?' Luke asked.

'Nope.'

'Why not?'

'Figured if I set a trap every time, and once folks found it, they'd be confident to take my money. If I didn't set a trap then maybe they'd spend a long time searching for something that wasn't there.'

'You're a clever son of a bitch, aren't you?' Luke said.

'He reads a lot,' Amos said.

'Where's the money in this outhouse?'

'Same place. Up in the roof.'

'If I send Burns here to get it and there's a trap then I'm asking Starling here to cut the old fellow's tongue out here and now. Understand?'

'If there's a snake in the outhouse I never put it there.'

Luke nodded. Then he turned to Burns and said, 'Go get the money. But be careful.'

        ★   ★   ★

There'd been five of them. *That* was the niggle. He'd watched them around town long enough, in the Bridge Hotel, here and there. Seeing who was who. And he'd counted five. Never altogether at one time . . . and that was the thing. They weren't together at one time now, there was four of them down there and the fifth . . .

'Hands up,' the fifth man said. 'Real slow, now.'

Sheriff Wagner recognized the man's

voice. Sure enough, as the feller rode into sight, he saw it was the man they called Rivers. Scarface. The leader of the gang.

'I should shoot you,' Rivers said. 'If it was Starling instead of me you'd probably already be dead.'

Wagner said, 'You. It was you all along.'

'This is what I want you to do, I want you to take out that Colt, real slow, and drop it on the ground. You even look like your finger is going near the trigger then I'm going to kill you. Then I'm going to go down there and kill your friends.'

Wagner did as he was told.

'Now the rifles, both of them. On the ground. Good. Now ride on, nice and slow down that slope. Don't give me any reason to shoot you.'

Wagner urged his horse forward. He wasn't certain but he thought he could see Jim Jackson looking back up the slope. He'd let Jim down. The fellow had changed a lot in the last week, had come good, and now Wagner had let him down. Wagner sighed. He'd been in a few scrapes before and maybe this wasn't the worst of them, maybe these boys would simply take Jim's money and ride on. That in itself would be a result; at least the town would be free of them.

But would they do that?

Would they feel comfortable knowing that no-one would be coming after them?

Wagner figured that were the positions reversed he'd expect someone to come after him. Which meant, if they felt the same, then the chances were these fellows would kill him, Amos, and Jim.

★   ★   ★

Jim's heart sank.

He hadn't known how he and Wagner would pull off a turnaround but he'd had no doubt they would. Now, up there on the slope, Wagner was coming down the hill in plain sight, and behind him was Scarface himself, holding a gun on Wagner.

Starling had spotted them, too.

'Boss is here,' he said. 'Looks like the sheriff, too.'

Luke said, 'Seems like they were planning another trap to me.'

'Yeah, reckon so.'

Just then Burns came round the side of the building with the second bag of money. It looked even heavier than the first.

'We're rich, boys,' he said. 'All of us.'

★   ★   ★

Rivers said, 'So how are we doing, boys?'

Luke Hamilton showed him the two bags of money they'd retrieved so far.

'Silver dollars and eagles, gold and national notes are good,' Rivers said. 'Any trouble?'

'Henry Slade is dead,' Starling said. 'Got bit by a snake.'

Starling looked across at Jim Jackson.

Jim Jackson shrugged as if to say *so be it*.

'No other trouble?'

'Nope.'

'Lucky for you boys I was riding rear,' Rivers said. 'Sheriff here was armed to the teeth.'

'You fellows won't get away with this,' Wagner said.

'Won't get away with what?' Rivers said. There was a relaxed air about him now. He looked down at those two bags of money and it was as if it was all he could do to keep from smiling. 'Can't say as we've done anything wrong.'

'Henry's dead. McCrae's dead. Southee's dead. And you're stealing somebody's money? I'd say the list is long enough for you all to swing.'

Amos added, 'They tore me from the hole, too. Banged me about and threatened to cut off my thumbs.'

'Just talk,' Starling said. 'And the reason we brought you along was to avoid the need for any violence. Figured

Shaky here was fond enough of you to do what we asked. I think we figured right.'

Rivers nodded. 'Anyway, Slade got bit by a snake, they just said. McRae — that bearded fellow, yes? — and the other one you mentioned. Nothing to do with us.'

Amos spat on the ground.

Wagner said, 'Expect a judge to believe that?'

'I'd expect a jury to need proof. And, on top of that, all this money . . . ' He waved his hands over the two bags. 'Stolen anyway.' He looked at Jim. 'Yes?'

Jim Jackson looked back at the man, at the way the lines around his eyes appeared to have lessened, at the tension that was no longer in the man's face, at the way his mouth was almost turned up in a smile. It was the relaxed look of victory.

'If all this money is enough to make you fellows move on, then take it and go,' he said.

Rivers looked back at Wagner. 'You see. We've done nothing wrong and even have the *owner's* blessing.'

Jim Jackson was thinking of McRae suspended there upside on that bridge. There was no blessing being given. He knew that if these guys moved on he would follow them. One way or another, this wasn't over.

'Maybe,' Rivers said, 'we will move on. Maybe not.'

But Jim saw Starling grinning and in the expression he knew that whatever they intended, leaving him and Wagner alive wasn't part of it. He thought about making a move for one of their guns. That Bridge fellow, not Burns, but the other fellow. He was quiet. He was just standing there by Amos. Bit of an unknown quantity. And Burns, well, in a moment he'd be off in another outhouse looking for another bag of money. That left the one called Luke Hamilton and Starling. And Rivers, too. But it was Hamilton and Starling he'd have to worry about. Could he snatch a gun from someone's belt and kill them all before they reacted?

Starling smiled at him as if he was reading Jim's thoughts. He actually placed a hand on the butt of his gun as if to say *don't even think about it, fellow*.

The one called Luke seemed pretty aware, too. Just the way he moved, he was never getting too close to Jim. It probably wasn't anything more than instinct, But it was good instinct and it pretty much ruined Jim's vague idea of snatching a weapon.

That said, there was still one chance left. The way the odds were, it might be enough.

'So,' Rivers said. 'Is there any more money?'

'Two bags,' Starling said. 'Or so he says. Might be worth double checking once we've got those.'

Rivers smiled and nodded. Jim shivered. He figured that they would hurt Amos just enough that if there was any more money Jim would tell them.

'Where's the next one?' Rivers asked.
'Just up the road,' Jim said.

★   ★   ★

The money was again in an outhouse.
This time the outhouse was one of
three that had been built in a row at
the rear of a building that looked like
it had once been the largest place in
town, save the mine. Jim Jackson
had assumed it was a hotel of some
description until he went inside when
he found, to some delight, that it had
actually been a theatre. There was even
a piano in there and when he first saw
it, he thought of the one back at the
Domino that the owners had hauled all
the way from Kansas when there'd been
one here, just a half day away. The
money was in the middle of the three
outhouses, all of which faced outwards,
away from the hotel.

The door to the outhouse swung
closed once Burns went in. A moment
later he came out holding the bag of

money in his hand.

He held it up, grinning.

And then he was blasted back against the outhouse door, a spray of blood arcing through the air, the money bag falling to the floor, spilling its contents, and as he hit the door and left a thick smear of blood from the back of his head, they heard the sharp sound of the gunshot that had killed him.

14

Rose had never seen boys who could run the way that Little Joe and Ghost did. They ran in the effortless way that only boys of a certain age can, not seeming to think about energy or exhaustion or tiring out, just running, and laughing, and getting excited every time the trail changed direction.

They'd already been miles ahead of her by the time Mannie saddled up a mare and sent her on her way. She'd told Mannie what had happened, that she was going after Amos. He said he'd have come too were it not for the fact that he was kicked in the nether regions by a grumpy stallion a couple of years ago and still couldn't sit on a horse for more than five minutes. And that was if the horse wasn't moving.

Out of town, and back on the trail, she could see the boys in the distance.

Tiny figures kicking up a cloud of dust as they ran. Once she caught up with them she managed to fit them both on her horse — it was a squeeze but both boys were thin and light. She couldn't help but wonder when either of them had last had a proper meal. They made good time despite Ghost jumping down every few minutes and looking at the ground.

'We're going to Santiago,' Ghost said at one point, more than an hour into their journey. 'There's nothing else between here and there.'

'Have you been there before?' Rose asked.

'Many times. I walk there on quiet days.'

After an age made longer by the frustration that they couldn't move faster, the trail started to wend its way upwards, into the hills, into the pinewoods. Another hour later, once they began to descend again, Rose felt something rising within her. It was as if a sixth sense was telling her: *You're*

243

here now. You've got that heavy gun strapped to your leg. What is it that you're going to do? It wasn't fear. It wasn't even nervousness. It was a place where fear and nervousness and anger and apprehension all met and smashed into each other. There was even revenge in there, she realized. Revenge against this damn wilderness that had taken Frankie from her.

'I hear talking,' Little Joe said.

Ghost said, 'Santiago's just down in the valley. I can hear them, too.'

The boys had better ears than her. Better eyes, too, for when she stopped the mare in the tree line and the boys jumped down, the first thing Little Joe said was, 'What's that?'

The second thing he said, answering his own question, was, 'Guns.'

★ ★ ★

Laidlaw let go of Amos's arm and dived to the ground. Both Starling and Hamilton crouched down, scampered for cover behind the building, and as they did so they scanned the hillside, looking up and down the road. Rivers looked shocked for a second, but then he too was running a jagged line for cover.

The sheriff and Jim both reached Amos at the same time.

Amos said, 'Gunshot? I've been shot at more times this last week than in the last year. The last five years.'

They pulled him to cover behind the same building as Starling and Rivers. Laidlaw had crawled across to a tin water trough that was empty, and red with rust despite the dryness of the atmosphere.

They heard the 'ting' of a bullet hitting the water trough before they heard the sound of the gunshot itself. In the seconds immediately after the shot, Laidlaw stood up and ran across to where everyone else was sheltering.

Rivers said, 'Who the hell is that?'

Starling said, 'They're up on the slope. Damn good shot whoever it is.'

He looked at Jim Jackson and added, 'Or lucky.'

Rivers said, 'Laidlaw, you keep these boys covered. Keep them at arm's length, too. They're slippery. Any of them looks like they might even think about doing something, shoot them.' He turned to Starling and Hamilton. 'Let's split, two left — me and Luke. Starling, you go right. Don't shoot each other, but whoever it is up there let's go and get them.'

Then Rivers took off his black coat, revealing a pistol belted to his waist.

'Go.'

⋆ ⋆ ⋆

She had killed a man.

What was it Jim had said? He wouldn't wish it on anyone. Well, maybe he was a better person than her because she didn't feel anything right now. Looking down the slope, seeing those men with guns clearly holding Amos and Jim and the sheriff at gunpoint, knowing what they were doing, knowing what they had done, she had simply taken one of those rifles that had been lying there abandoned on the ground and she had imagined it was twenty years ago and she was shooting a rabbit for supper.

No, that wasn't strictly true.

She'd used those old days as a reminder of technique and confidence. But what she was *thinking* was about sending those sons of bitches right to hell.

'Heavens above,' Little Joe said. 'I didn't know you could shoot, Miss Golde.'

The men below were all hiding now. Her second shot had been a bit wild. She wasn't sure what to do next.

She saw two of the men dart from cover, rushing out from behind a big building and racing across the open ground to her right. By the time she had raised the gun they were hidden from view again. Then she saw another man doing the same but to her left. She raised the gun again and even fired a shot but it wasn't even close to where the man had been, let alone to where he now was. As she lowered the rifle she saw the two men on the right burst from cover again and make it to another building, a closer building.

Little Joe was watching, too.

'They're coming for us,' he said.

* * *

Starling smiled as he dashed from one piece of cover to the next. The truth was he was getting a little impatient down there in this goddamn ghost town. Get the money and go was his opinion. Well, get the money and shoot these locals, maybe drop the bodies in one of those outhouse holes and go. He'd have liked to have gone up against Shaky just to prove to himself that he really could outgun the drunk. He wouldn't have admitted it to Shaky but the fellow had looked fast back in the street a few days ago. But it wasn't going to turn out that way. This was second-best — hunting down whoever was up there with a rifle.

Starling held his Colt in his right hand as he ran. Once a bullet echoed across the valley and he thought he heard the whistle of the lead through the air, but it wasn't close enough for him to be sure.

He made it to the last building — an adobe house — in the town. Ahead of him was a stretch of open ground and then the slope up to the trees.

For fifty yards, maybe more, there was no cover. But across to his right, moving away from where he wanted to be, there was another hut, and over there the valley started to narrow and turn.

He waited, and over to his left he saw Hamilton break cover. A moment later the rifle barked again, and then Starling was up and running, sprinting for the cover of the more distant building.

* * *

'I counted three,' Rose said. 'Two to the right, one to the left.'

Ghost was holding the six-gun they had found, and Little Joe had the other rifle. They were all staring out of the trees at the scene below. But it wouldn't be long before the three men coming up after them would be in the trees.

'We should hide,' Little Joe said.

'Or ride straight down there,' Ghost said. 'There can't be but one man left down there.'

It was an idea, Rose thought. But the three of them on the one horse, working their way down the slope? It would be too easy a shot.

'You're right, Joe,' she said. 'Boys, go into the woods. Keep quiet. And when you see these men . . . ' She let the words hang.

'Kill them,' Ghost said.

The boys vanished, Ghost to the left, Joe to the right.

She would hold her ground a little longer. Her position was good. You never know, she thought, I might be able to end it from here.

She saw one of the men break cover to her right. He was already working his way up the slope, diving behind a fallen tree now. She fired at him and immediately worked the action again and even as she did so he was moving again.

Over to her left more movement. She turned and raised the gun, fired again.

'Got him!' she said, as the man stumbled and fell. But a moment later he was up again and running for cover. 'Damn.'

She worked the action again, but the gun was empty.

⋆   ⋆   ⋆

The shot, the fact that the closeness of it caused him to stumble, and the even greater fact that it could have killed him, made Starling angry. Once in cover he looked at his gun, spun the chamber, checked the hammer action. It was good to go. It was *always* good to go.

There was a dry stream bed that came down from the tree line about twenty yards to his right. In winter, or at least in the brief rainy season that preceded winter around these parts, maybe that channel would have fed a steady stream of water down into the town. For now, it offered him enough cover to get up to the trees. The blue-tinged grass grew high upon the edges of the stream bed, and the water cascading down the hill over thousands of years had carved out steps in the bed.

He waited a while, waiting for whoever was up there to shoot again. But when a shot never came and his patience and anger started to ebb, he dashed for the river bed, zig-zagging the best he could, his spurs tinkling, and his back itching where a bullet might take him.

But no bullet came.

Then he was working his way uphill, breathing heavily, but looking forward to the moment he would find whoever had the audacity to try and kill him.

Ghost heard the man before he could see him. The heavy breathing, the snapping of dry branches, once or twice a whispered curse.

He stood behind a tree, pressed up against its trunk and held the six-gun in both hands. His heart was breathing rapidly and the gun felt heavy in his hands. He tried to hold his breath and listen, but when he wasn't breathing his heart and the rush of blood in his ears overpowered everything. So he breathed again and he tried to picture the man working his way through the trees, but instead what he saw was a man in uniform, many men in uniform, waves of them on horses coming racing through their small camp. He saw his mother crouched down by their cooking fire, could even smell the roasting rabbit, and then he saw her looking up with fear in her eyes, reaching for him, but being knocked aside by a horse, blood bursting from her forehead, and a scream erupting from her lips.

The horse's hind leg caught him and a darkness came over him and when he next opened his eyes, the sun had moved in the sky and it was quiet, so quiet, save for someone crying nearby. He started crying, too. They were all dead. His mother, his father, his friends, their mothers and their fathers. He had done nothing. He hadn't even seen any of their faces. It was a vision — a nightmare — that came to him often. All his life he had heard stories of the great — and awful — deeds of his people. People were terrified of them. Soldiers were in awe of them. His people had been great and brave, and yet he had done nothing except not even see the enemy and then wake up crying.

Somewhere behind him he heard the crackle of someone stepping on dry leaves.

He stepped out from behind the tree, raised the gun, and fired towards the sound.

Starling heard the whistle of the bullet and the retort of the gun at about the same time. The bullet ploughed into a tree somewhere behind him.

He crouched low and when someone fired a second bullet at him he saw their movement ahead of him.

The angle was risky — Rivers and Hamilton were over in that general direction. But what was the chance of hitting them? They probably hadn't made as good time as him, and if they had anything about them they'd be low down and behind trees, too.

When that someone ahead of him tried their luck with a third bullet, Starling decided enough was enough.

He shot at the movement ahead of him. Four bullets. Bang, bang. Bang. Bang.

Then he stopped and he listened.

And when he heard nothing he slowly reloaded his gun with four fresh cartridges and he edged forwards.

Rose heard the gunfire to her left. First of all three shots, quite a gap between them. Then four shots, very fast. It reminded her of the way Jim had shot back in the copse behind her house.

It went quiet again and in that quiet she held her breath. Even the birds had stopped singing. She could hear the breeze rustling through the leaves but that was it. She wanted to cry out, ask the boys if they were all right, but that would give away her position. So she stayed still, hard up against a tree, and she listened.

Suddenly there was movement to her right, rustling that was more than the wind in the trees.

She raised her gun — Jim's gun. McRae's gun. It felt too heavy in her hand. She had her own little parlour gun tucked inside her jacket, but this was no moment for a toy gun. The thought was absurd. Jim Jackson would have laughed at her.

She steadied the revolver with both hands and peered into the tangled shadows of the woods, watching for movement through the ferns and the low branches and the leaves.

★   ★   ★

Luke Hamilton came up behind the kid.

Give the boy credit, he thought, he didn't look scared. No, instead there was a look of fierce determination in the kid's posture.

It was the kid from around town, the water boy.

Luke watched him for a few minutes and then quietly worked his way around the back of the boy.

When he was close enough he pressed the barrel of his revolver against the boy's neck and whispered, 'Don't move, son.'

The boy did move, but it was just an involuntary jerk of his head.

'Drop the gun,' Luke said.

The boy did as he was told. But then he looked around at Hamilton and said, 'Jim Jackson's gonna get you, mister. You can kill me, but Jim'll kill you.'

'I'm not going to kill you,' Hamilton said. 'You're just a kid.'

'I'd kill you if you hadn't snuck up on me.'

'Well, next time you're hiding from someone don't wear a bright yellow hat that a feller can see from a hundred yards away. Now, walk in front of me, real slow now.'

Rose almost pulled the trigger. In fact, she was already applying enough pressure to the trigger to have fired her little gun but this one needed a lot more force.

It was Little Joe who stepped out from the trees. Little Joe with someone behind him — that young fellow from around town who had been offering to look out for and protect people against coming trouble, including herself — and that someone looked like he had a gun pressed against Little Joe's back.

'Drop your gun, lady,' the man said. 'You don't, I'll shoot the boy and then you.'

'Don't do it, Missy Rose,' Little Joe said. 'He already told me he won't kill a boy.'

She realized she was pointing her own gun right at the man. If it had been a rifle and she was able to aim it properly and take her time, it may have been a shot that she could have made. Though she knew it wasn't one she would have dared, not with Little Joe in the firing line. But she didn't lower the gun. It was all she had left between them — her and Little Joe and Ghost — and these men.

'Drop it,' the man said.

Now another man appeared out of the woods. The older man with the scar on his face. He looked out of breath.

'He won't shoot a kid,' Little Joe said.

The man with the scar also had a gun. He pointed it at Rose. 'Do as Luke says.'

The gun was getting very heavy in

her hands. She knew she either had to fire it, try and hit both of them right now, or lower it. Give up. Surrender. The thought crossed her mind that the reason she was still out here, not living it up in San Francisco, was because she had never given up, never surrendered.

She felt her finger pressurising the trigger.

'I'll kill you,' Scarface said. 'Your finger so much as twitches again and I'll kill you. He don't like to kill children and I don't like to kill women. But we both will.'

She looked from one man to the other, and she looked at Little Joe and she felt the weight of the gun in her hand.

She breathed out slowly.

She lowered the gun.

15

Back in the Texas convict leasing system, the man who had tortured Jim, mentally and physically, more than any other had been named Webster T. Ellington. Webster insisted that all the prisoners addressed him as Captain, visitors could call him Mr Ellington, and his bosses got away with Webb. On the day that Jim Jackson was released the Captain walked with him to the gate. There was a look of disappointment in the Captain's eyes, maybe, Jim thought because they hadn't driven him to the point where he would run or attack an officer or do something, anything that would have given them the excuse to shoot him dead or hang him.

'What you do,' the Captain said, 'is you leave Texas and you never come back. You understand?'

Jim Jackson nodded and said he understood. He had no intention of setting foot in Texas again. Texas was, as far as Jim was concerned, hell with a capital H.

'The bat is waiting. You know what I'm saying?'

Just the mention of the bat was enough to weaken Jim's knees and cause him to have to squeeze his stomach muscles tight to prevent accidents.

'Folks above have considered it appropriate to buy you a ticket on a stagecoach north,' the Captain said. 'Me, I'd have made you walk and I'd have ridden alongside you and God help you if you'd have stumbled or stopped. But . . . You get on that stage and you don't get off until they kick you off, *comprendez*?'

'I understand.'

'They'll kick you off at the border. You'll be in the Territories then. Somebody else's problem. I forecast you'll be dead before nightfall.'

Jim said, 'I had . . . I had belongings when I came here.'

The Captain laughed so hard that spittle had landed on Jim's face.

'In a way,' the Captain said. 'I hope you come back. I'd love to use the bat on you again. No-one else screams the way you do.'

Jim stared at the man.

'Wagon over there is waiting for you. Don't forget, you take one step inside Texas again and I'll be waiting.'

Jim exited the prison through the wire and iron gate. He took a deep breath and five steps, and then he turned and said, 'Thanks for the memories, Tex.'

At the border the stagecoach driver was as good as his word. He pulled the stagecoach to a halt, dropped down from the riding board and opened the door. There was just Jim Jackson and one other fellow, a writer who had spent the whole journey asking questions. There'd been no need for Jim to enhance his prison experiences but the fellow had kept telling him not to make it up, to tell the truth. The driver told

Jim that this was as far as his ticket went and that if he walked towards the setting sun he'd find a town sooner or later.

As they pulled away, the writer fellow had leaned out of the window and had thrown Jim a half-filled water skin.

Jim Jackson sat on his haunches until the stagecoach was out of sight and the dust of its departure was beginning to settle.

Then he vomited in fear, bringing up nothing but bile because they hadn't wasted prison food on a man who was being released, and he turned and stepped back into Texas.

Heading back to get his money was the most frightening thing Jim had ever done. But Texas had taken everything from him and he knew that the only way he could stay alive in this world was with that money.

It had taken him a week, and when he finally made it back to the border — dressed as a Mexican peasant and riding a mule for which he'd paid the price of a stallion he vowed he'd never go there again.

It was about then that he started shaking.

Now he looked at the three men coming down the hill, with Rose and Little Joe staggering along in front of them. He looked at the three bags of money on the ground, at Laidlaw holding that gun on them and grinning.

When Rose was within speaking distance she said, 'I'm sorry.'

Amos said, 'Rose?'

Little Joe was crying. 'They shot Ghost,' he said.

The sheriff said, 'You sons of bitches' and took a step towards the party approaching them, but Laidlaw ratcheted the action on his gun and told Wagner to stand still, that if someone hadn't shot Burns dead then Ghost would still be alive.

When Rivers came close enough to be heard without raising his voice he said, 'Laidlaw's right. You guys brought that on the kid, what's his name?

Ghost. Now, we're almost done.' He looked at Jim. 'You said there were four bags of money?'

'There is.'

'Where's the last one?'

Jim said, 'It's the biggest bag. Biggest by far. It's in the mine.'

16

Jim Jackson said it was no good him telling them where the bag was. It was dark in there, pitch black. He said he'd hidden the bag in a crevice and that there were many crevices. He knew which one — but how could he describe it? He said there were a couple of pits in there, too. Deep pits filled with water and he wasn't sure how deep. Then he said he was happy to crawl in there with Laidlaw. Or Hamilton. Or Starling. He'd go first, or second. Whatever they wanted. But it was tight and low and he didn't want anyone panicking and blaming him if they got stuck.

They talked about it, Rivers and Luke Hamilton and Starling, standing in that big store room looking at the door that led into the rock face. The door was open and the darkness beyond was pitch black because no-one had lit any lanterns. In fact, Jim had hidden the kerosene lamps a few days ago. Whoever went in there was going in blind. The room they stood in was gloomy and shadowy, but the mine looked like solid coal.

After their discussion Rivers said, 'This is how it's going to be. You go in there alone and you bring the bag out. You yell when you're coming and you throw that bag out. Then you come out with your hands up.'

'I can do that.'

'Any sign . . . any hint . . . in fact, if I even get just a feeling that you might be double crossing us I'm going to shoot them all. Understand?'

Comprendez?

Starling was standing, gun in hand close to Rose. Laidlaw was next to Wagner. Hamilton had a hand on Little Joe's shoulder, but Little Joe was also holding the sheriff's hand, Amos was standing on his own, but Rivers had a gun in his hand and was close to the blind man.

'I understand.'

'How long's it going to take you?'

'It's pitch black and it's a long tunnel. I have to crawl quite a way and then find the money — '

'You said you knew where it was.'

'I do. I still need to find it, and dig it out.'

'You do this every time you need money?' Starling said.

'No. This is my main stash. Haven't had to touch it in a long time.'

'How long?' Rivers asked.

'How long since I've had to touch this stash?'

'How long's it gonna take you?'

'Thirty minutes.'

'You've got twenty,' Rivers said. 'Then I shoot Amos. Five minutes later I shoot the sheriff.'

There was no money. What there was was the gun that he had bought at Mulligan's. He had hidden it behind a rock in the main cavern. If they had sent someone in with him he would have retrieved the gun from behind that rock and in the light coming down from the natural airshaft he would have shot them dead.

But they'd sent him on his own.

It was perfect. A final card to play. An ace right there in a real to goodness hole.

He didn't need to crawl and he didn't need light. He ran into the cave and, crouching down, scampered along the tunnel towards the cavern.

In the cavern he quickly found his gun and he climbed up the ladder that he'd put in place a few days before.

Then he worked his way along the rock-face, back down into the valley floor, and into the mine building behind them.

It was like heading back into Texas.

⋆   ⋆   ⋆

Amos heard Jim Jackson coming. One of the horses outside snorted and Amos heard the old plank walk outside groan with the weight of someone treading on it. A moment later he heard the door hinges squeak.

It seemed like hardly any time had gone by. Whatever Jim was up to he, Amos, wanted to give him every bit of help he could.

'My belly . . . ' he said.

'What about your belly?' someone asked him.

'You guys pulled me off the hole hours ago and never let me go. I can't hold it in no more.'

'We'll soon be done.'

'Soon might not be soon enough.' He pulled a face and sighed. 'Jesus,' he said. 'It really does hurt. Sorry, Rose,' he added, and let out a long flatulent explosion. 'That's better.' He started to laugh. 'Your faces,' he said.

'You can't see our faces,' someone said.

'I can imagine them,' Amos said, and started to laugh, as loud and as long as he could whilst keeping it as natural as he was able.

★ ★ ★

Jim Jackson stepped through the door, his gun already raised. Before anyone realized he was there he shot Rivers in the forehead. The man dropped, dead before he hit the ground. Jim's second shot killed Luke Hamilton and it was as he was swinging his gun towards Laidlaw that he realized his big mistake.

He should have taken Starling first.

He'd gone for the leader, Rivers. It should have been a good tactic. In that other life when he'd been part of Hans Freidlich's gang, Hans had always said if a group looks like they're preparing to fight back then shoot the leader. It had never been necessary, but it made sense.

Right now it had been a mistake. He had shot Scarface and then he had shot Hamilton because Hamilton had been the next in line as he had turned his gun in an arc. And even as he squeezed his trigger and shot Laidlaw, his bullet taking the man in the chest and knocking him backwards, blood spraying in a semi-circle in the air like water from a horse shaking its mane after a storm, he knew he'd got the order wrong.

Starling was the fast one. The *fastest* one.

Starling was the one that was born to this. From the corner of his eye he saw Starling's gun already pointing at him. He saw Starling's finger turning white as he applied pressure to the trigger.

He's faster than me, Jim Jackson thought.

He heard the sound of a shot that wasn't his own and waited for the bullet to punch into him.

★   ★   ★

It wasn't like Amos to behave like that. In all the years that she had known him his manners had always been impeccable, And that laughing, that didn't sound like the way Amos laughed. He was talking too loudly, too. She didn't quite know what he was up to.

But he was up to something.

And something was about to happen.

She watched Amos and she watched Rivers. She ran her eyes over everyone and they were all looking into the darkness of the mine.

There was tension in the air. It felt as if a lightning storm was about to hit. Was it only she that could feel it?

She reached inside her jacket and felt for that tiny little parlour gun that she'd had there all day long. It was loaded. Just one bullet. She wrapped her hand around the gun, felt for the trigger.

She heard a soft footstep somewhere in the room behind her.

And she realized that the one next to her could feel it, too. He was turning, looking around, his body tensing.

She pulled the tiny gun from inside her jacket. It was almost hidden in her hand.

She started to raise the gun.

After that it all happened in a blur. Jim Jackson coming into that storeroom, gun in hand, already blazing away. One shot, two shots. Blood in the air and two men down dying so quickly that they probably didn't even know they were dead yet. Then as Jim was swinging that gun towards the third man, Starling was raising his gun, aiming now at Jim Jackson, smiling, now grinning, and as Jim Jackson shot the third man and started to turn towards Starling, Starling's grin turned into a laugh, a deadly laugh, and she pressed her parlour gun against Starling's neck and pulled the trigger.

★   ★   ★

No-one spoke for what seemed like an age. Then Amos said, 'My ears are hurting. Someone please tell me what just happened here?'

Still nobody said anything.

Jim Jackson was looking at Rose. He was breathing heavily. She couldn't take her eyes off him. It was as if the moment she moved her gaze everything would become real. The sheriff, too, was breathing hard. His lips were pursed as if he was about to whistle and his chest heaved as he breathed and blew air through his lips.

'You all dead?' Amos said.

'Jim and Rose killed them all,' Little Joe Grubber said. 'You should've seen it.'

Amos smiled.

'I heard it and I imagined it. Is everyone OK?'

'We are now,' Sheriff Wagner said.

Rose stepped forward towards Jim. She nodded at him. Every question she needed to ask was in that nod. He nodded back. They were OK. They were all OK.

Amos said, 'I don't mean to labour the point but there's been a lot of talk of outhouses this last hour. Would someone mind taking me to one?'

17

Amos said, 'When I was a kid, no more'n seven or eight years old, me and another boy name of Moose Branningan — well, Moose wasn't his real name. I don't recall his real name. Not sure I ever knew it. But he had ears, you know? Big ears. Anyways, me and Moose, we found a dead body out in the holler a few miles back from where we lived.'

They were on the plank walk outside Rose's front door. Amos had a cup of strong coffee in his hand. Rose was sitting on the chair by her door and Little Joe Grubber was sitting on the top step that led up to Rose's porch, his feet splayed out in the street. Little Joe wore a black hat now. When Jim had asked him what had happened to the yellow one, Little Joe told him that he'd given it to a fellow for a dime. Little Joe had looked a little sad and had said if he'd been wearing a black hat things might have been different.

Jim's horse was in the street. Jim was leaning on the railing alongside Amos. He had a coffee, too. His was balanced on the railing whilst he smoked a cigarette.

Across the street some fellows were walking by with a long ladder.

Amos said, 'This dead man — we couldn't tell what he'd died from — but he wasn't buried. I think he may have been shot or stabbed. There was blood coming through this blanket they wrapped him in. Anyway, Moose dared me to open the blanket and look at him.'

Little Joe looked up and said, 'Ain't much of a dare. I ain't scared of no bloody dead man.'

'There was flies and all,' Amos said. 'But I reached down and opened the blanket.'

Amos paused, sipped from his coffee, and stared sightlessly across the street. Today was a new bandage day.

'And?' Rose said.

'You know what?' Amos said.

'We're waiting,' Jim said.

'That feller had a silver dollar on each eye. Leastways, I remember it as a silver dollar.' Amos laughed. 'Probably was a nickel. Anyway, me and Moose, we couldn't believe our luck.'

'You took the coins?' Rose said.

'Damn right,' Amos said. 'If I recall, Moose bought himself a real to good-ness genuine sheriff's badge from a feller in town.'

'And you?' Rose asked.

'I . . . I gave mine to my mother. We didn't have much. I told her I found the money. She was all for asking round town to see if anyone had lost the money. I told her where I found it, but I never told her the truth.'

He sipped his coffee again.

Across the street Father Thornley and Freeman Grainger walked in the same direction as the men with the ladder. They raised their hands. Jim nodded back.

'Is that it?' Little Joe asked. 'Is that the end of the story?'

'Not quite,' Amos said. 'See Moose got killed. He got killed by a feller with a gun and a lucky shot. He got shot in the eye.'

'In the eye?' Little Joe said.

'Uh-huh.'

'And I guess I knew,' Amos said. 'That one day . . . See, what we did when we stole the money off that feller's eyes . . . I knew that one day I'd get shot in the eye, too. Except I wasn't shot. I had the Apache, that's what I had. But it happened because me and Moose took money from a dead man's eyes.'

'Wow,' Little Joe said. 'That's a good story.'

'I'm not sure the world works that way, Amos,' Rose said.

'Maybe. Maybe not,' Amos said. 'But why take the risk?'

* * *

Jim Jackson had already decided to give the money away before he'd heard Amos's tale. But the story reinforced his decision and though he didn't say it aloud, he kind of agreed with what Amos was saying. Rivers had said it back up in Santiago. It was stolen money. In a way it was as cursed as those coins from a dead man's eyes. It was just all of his dreams had been built on that money. He had gone through hell for that money and he had risked hell again to get it back. To let it go had never been an option.

But the last few weeks had changed all that. He knew he had to let the money go in order to be able to live.

So he'd pledged enough of it to the church so that they could get a bell — they were measuring up this morning, those fellers with a ladder, and Thornley and Grainger taking notes down at ground level. He'd paid for a good burial for Ghost and he'd given Little Joe enough money to order in some extra buckets and a supply of soft paper to really get his little businesses flying. Neither Rose nor Amos wanted any of the money, and he understood that, so what little remained he put in a small pouch and he carried with him. It wasn't spending money, it was what he called 'right time' money. Sooner or later the right time to use it or give it would appear.

* * *

Jim Jackson finished his coffee, put the cup down on the rail, and said, 'I guess it's time.'

Amos turned his bandages towards Jim and said simply, 'So long, pardner.'

'Amos.'

'You say you're coming back?'

'Yep. Reckon this is home these days.'

'In that case I'll see you then,' Amos said and held out his hand.

After they had shaken hands Amos said, 'Think I might just walk out back. Save having to watch you ride out. Never could stand goodbyes.'

Rose said, 'It wasn't as bad as you made out. Killing someone, I mean.'

'You saved my life.'

'*You* saved all of our lives.'

'I guess when the people you kill are bad people and they are planning on killing you then maybe God doesn't hit you so hard afterwards. With remorse and stuff, I mean.'

'I don't feel remorse,' she said. 'In some ways, I'm glad those men came to town. I mean, we got you back, didn't we?'

She smiled and there was sadness in her smile. She looked at his horse, all laden up.

'I'm coming back,' he said. 'I promised Amos I'd bring some new books. I also promised him that you'd finish *Moll Flanders* for him. Will you do that?'

'Of course.'

'You be careful,' she said.

They hugged and she kissed his hair

and then she kissed his cheek and then his lips. There were tears in her eyes.

'Go on,' she said. 'Before I cry.'

Jim climbed on his horse, looked back at Rose and then he pressed his heels into the horse's flanks.

Little Joe jumped to his feet and ran alongside the horse.

'You really going to break some fellers out of prison, Jim?'

'Shush,' Jim said, smiling. 'You mustn't let anyone know. Especially the sheriff there.'

Wagner was waiting outside his office.

'When you come back, son, there's a job for you here. I can guarantee there ain't a feller in town who won't vote for you if you want to be the next sheriff of Parker's Crossing.'

'I will be back. But we've got a fine sheriff. Folks here don't need me.'

'They got a sheriff who's feeling his age. That's what they've got. I might even go so far as to offer myself up as your deputy.'

'You got it all planned out, huh? You aiming on putting Julio out of work?'

'A man's got to have a plan. Anyway, the town's growing. A sheriff like you could use at least two deputies.'

The sheriff winked at Jim Jackson.

'We'll see,' Jim said.

'Anyways, you ride safe and you come back and tell me all about it.'

'I'll do that, pardner.'

He pressed his heels again and this time Little Joe didn't run with him, he stayed there standing next to the sheriff the way he had been back in Santiago when all the killing had gone down.

*   *   *

Jim Jackson adjusted Sam McRae's gun on his hip. He'd spent some time searching for the gun up on the rise above Santiago. It had been there in the undergrowth where Rose had dropped it.

He thought now of what McRae had told him.

There's a fellow talking about killing a Texas Ranger during a train robbery.

He's been living it up and talking loose. He even supposedly mentioned you by name. Gentleman Jim Jackson.

There'd been a Texas Ranger on the train. Jim didn't know why — maybe it had been purely coincidence. But halfway through the robbery the Ranger had pulled a gun on Jim Jackson. Jim Jackson had raised his hands and said, 'You got me, boss.' But beneath the bandana covering most of his face Jim had been smiling. He could see one of the other fellows sneaking up on the Ranger from behind. Just as the Ranger started to rise Jim's fellow train robber dropped an empty feed bag over the Ranger's head, and knocked the gun from his hand.

If that had been all that had occurred then maybe none of what happened over the next ten years would have happened.

But then another masked man had stepped up and shot the Ranger in the head, through the burlap sack.

It had been point blank range.

It had been an execution.

And amidst a carriage full of screaming people it had been the moment it all changed.

Over in Leyton, Texas, there's a fellow named Jack Anderson who's been talking about a killing he did during a train robbery some twelve years ago.

Jim had always said there was something wrong about that killing, something that didn't add up.

It was time to go and see Jack Anderson of Leyton, Missouri. But there was something else to do first. Maybe some folks who might want to ride along to Leyton.

McRae had said: 'Word is the fellow has been talking about how he gave up four members of the gang — the rest of the gang. You know what I'm saying. There were four of you jailed.'

They'd been a team. OK, a gang. Freidlich's gang. But until that day they hadn't killed anyone — and they'd

287

worked well together. If any of them were going through what he'd been through, well, he wanted to know about it. Wanted to help them. And if any of them were still going through it then God help him, he was going to break them out. And if a fellow by the name of Webster T. Ellington, 'Captain' to his prisoners wanted to threaten him with the bat again, well, that was a meeting Jim Jackson would look forward to.

McRae's gun comfortable on his hip, he rode forwards. He stopped at the edge of town, wheeled his horse once, and waved just on the off-chance that there was anyone watching him leave.

Then he turned and rode towards Texas.

Other titles in the
Linford Western Library:

LONELY IS THE HUNTER

Dale Graham

When outlaw Caleb Ollinger and his gang stop in the New Mexico town of Carrizozo, a few drinks and a game of poker suddenly turn into a double killing. The gambler who was caught cheating matters little, but an innocent boy plowed down by Ollinger was the son of New Mexico's territorial governor. Bounty hunter Chance Newcombe is hired to bring the killer in, though he hasn't reckoned on competition from an old comrade who's been promised amnesty for his past crimes if he secures the prize first . . .